THE CONTEST KID
STRIKES AGAIN

THE CONTEST KID STRIKES AGAIN

another hilarious Hawkins adventure

BARBARA BROOKS WALLACE
Illustrated by Gloria Kamen

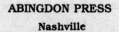

ABINGDON PRESS

Nashville

THE CONTEST KID STRIKES AGAIN

This book is printed on acid-free paper.

Library of Congress Cataloging in Publication Data

WALLACE, BARBARA BROOKS, 1922-
  The contest kid strikes again.
  SUMMARY: Harvey's love of anything free
continues to lead him into countless escapades and
dilemmas.
  [1. Collectors and collection—Fiction] I.
Kamen, Gloria. II. Title.
PZ7.W1547Co   [Fic]   79-24197

ISBN 0-687-09591-3

Formerly published under ISBN 0-687-09590-5

Printed in the United States of America

For three very special friends
Donny, Jimmy, and Billy Dawes
With love from Aunt Bobbie

Contents

Contents

I

Little Old-Fashioned Puppies

"Wow!" exclaimed Woody Woodruff. "I'll bet there're a zillion billion marbles in that jar. What do you bet, Harvey?"

Harvey Small and his friend Woody were standing in front of one of their favorite places in town, Bunce's Pet Store, and had been doing one of their favorite things, talking to some cute, wiggly puppies through the plate-glass window. Today, however, there was something in Bunce's window besides the usual kittens, puppies, or rabbits. Today the window featured a huge glass jar filled with marbles, and the person who came closest to guessing the correct number of marbles would win one of the puppies.

"Come on, Harvey," Woody insisted. "What do you bet?"

"Gee, Woody, what's the use of betting if when you win you can't even take home the prize?" Harvey said gloomily.

"Look, Harvey, supposing you just plain old won a puppy and nobody had to go out and buy it, and then you brought it through the front door without telling anybody ahead of time." Woody lowered his voice, getting very dramatic. "There you'd be, coming in with this cute little puppy in your arms. Your mom and dad would see you, dripping tears all over this puppy, and they would see how much you wanted to keep it. Do you think they'd make you give it back then?"

Harvey sighed. "Are you kidding, Woody?"

"Well, they let you keep Hawkins when you won *him* in a contest, didn't they? They *made* you keep him, Harvey."

"Yeah, but Betsy didn't start sneezing when she got within six feet of him, either. English gentlemen's gentlemen don't give people allergies, Woody. Anyway, I only won him for a month, not forever."

"Yeah, that's right," said Woody.

12

"And you remember that time I fell out of a tree and nearly killed myself?"

"I thought you only broke your big toe."

"Well, I *could* have killed myself," said Harvey. "Anyway, I thought they'd be so grateful I wasn't dead they'd give me a puppy or a kitten then. They got me a goldfish."

"Maybe they weren't very grateful," Woody suggested.

"I guess not," said Harvey.

"I remember that goldfish," Woody said. "It was a neat funeral you had for him, Harvey."

"Yeah," said Harvey.

They gave a few moments of respectful silence to the memory of Harvey's goldfish.

"Well, even if you don't want the prize, you could still try to guess the number of marbles," Woody said. "Then if you did win, and I didn't, you could give the puppy to me."

"What do you want with a puppy?" Harvey asked. "You've already got Blazer. Your mom and dad probably wouldn't let *you* keep one, either."

"Oh, I'd just give it to my sister and say it was a birthday present," Woody replied airily. "Then Gwendolyn would have to take care of it, but I'd get to play with it! Come on, Harvey, let's each guess a number and then go in and tell Mr. Bunce."

"We-e-ell," said Harvey. He hated the thought of

winning something he couldn't keep; but, after all, it was a free contest—and for Harvey Small, the Free Thing King, free was free. Besides, the Smalls lived across the street from the Woodruffs, so if Woody won the puppy, Harvey would probably get to play with it almost as much as Woody. So why not guess?

"We-e-ell, okay, I will. But it's not any zillion billion, Woody. I'd say it was more like—" Harvey studied the marbles in the jar—"more like about five hundred."

"Five hundred!" exploded Woody. "You're crazy, Harvey. It's gotta be at least—" Woody studied the marbles, too—"at least two thousand."

They stood outside the window for quite a while arguing about the number, and then finally went inside to make their report to Mr. Bunce.

"Well, well, well," said Mr. Bunce. "I expected you two in here much sooner. But I can see from the appearance of your heads that you were down visiting Charlie the barber and getting your hair cut this morning."

"We weren't getting it cut, Mr. Bunce," Harvey said quickly. "We were getting it—uh—*styled* by Sharles the hair stylist. He pronounces it Sharles now, like in French."

"Well, it's still the same old Charlie-the-barber haircut, as far as I can see," said Mr. Bunce.

"Humph! What does he mean, giving himself such airs?"

"Oh, he's not airing himself," Woody said. "He was in hard times, Mr. Bunce, and he changed his name to try to get more business."

"Well, has business improved?" asked Mr. Bunce.

"He says it has—a whole lot," replied Harvey.

"Then good for him!" exclaimed Mr. Bunce. "You know, I've been away for a while, and I'm badly in need of a haircut myself. But if you boys' haircuts are any sample, then I won't need to worry. I'm sure that Sharles the hair stylist is still giving the same old Charlie-the-barber haircuts, no matter what he calls himself."

While Mr. Bunce was talking, he was unlocking a drawer behind the counter and pulling out a large tablet of yellow paper and a pencil stub. "Now, boys, I'm sure you're here to make a guess at the marbles. At least, Woody is. No point in your guessing, Harvey, since you couldn't keep the puppy if you did win. Your little sister can't come within whistling distance of puppies, or anything covered in fur or feathers, without sneezing her head off."

"I know, Mr. Bunce," Harvey said, "but I want to guess anyway. If I win, I'll give the puppy to

Woody, and he'll give it to Gwendolyn for a birthday present."

"Well, I see you boys have it all figured out. So let's have your guesses." Mr. Bunce licked his pencil point, prepared to write.

"I guess five hundred fifty," said Harvey.

Mr. Bunce noted Harvey's name and his number on the yellow tablet.

"Make mine one thousand," said Woody. "No, make it nine hundred. Did you say five hundred fifty, Harvey?"

"That's what Harvey said, Woody," said Mr. Bunce, getting impatient.

"Okay, okay!" Woody scratched his head nervously. "Make mine *eight* hundred, Mr. Bunce. No, I mean, make it—"

"Eight hundred has been registered by your name on the yellow tablet, Woody," said Mr. Bunce wearily. "I can't stand here all day while you make up your mind. Now you boys can just look around the store while I start cleaning out these hamster cages." He locked the yellow tablet back up in the drawer.

"May we watch, Mr. Bunce?" Harvey asked.

"I suppose so," replied Mr. Bunce, "as long as Woody stops worrying about those numbers. But speaking of watching, look who's out there watching the puppies through the window."

"That's Mayor Paddle, isn't it?" said Woody. "Wow! I wonder if he's going to come in and guess the number of marbles. I bet he'd like to win a puppy."

"I doubt it," said Mr. Bunce. "Do you see that young man with the mayor?"

Harvey and Woody nodded.

"Well, that happens to be P. M. Heister, the mayor's new assistant and chief adviser for his forthcoming campaign. Mr. Heister is all hepped up on modernizing everything, and he really has the mayor's ear. Why, I'll bet they're out there right now thinking about how they can make me modernize my storefront. Maybe they don't like that old-fashioned preserve jar sitting there full of old-fashioned marbles. Or maybe they even want to modernize those little old-fashioned puppies!"

"Gee, how do you modernize a puppy?" Harvey asked.

"Beats me," said Mr. Bunce. "But if there's a way, you can bet that P. M. Heister will think of it. You know, I don't understand how somebody like that young man can be related to a nice old lady like Mrs. Moseley."

Harvey's eyes widened. "Is he her *son*, Mr. Bunce?"

"Oh no, Harvey, nothing like that. More like a

fifth cousin ten times removed, I hear, but related, nonetheless."

"Hawkins has never said anything about him," Harvey said. "Do you suppose he knows Mr. Heister?"

"No, I don't suppose he does," replied Mr. Bunce. "Pass me that sack of hamster feed, please, Harvey. You can fill the watering can at the sink, Woody. Now, let's see, where was I?" He paused to pull on his ear. "Oh, yes—Mr. Heister. Well, he wasn't here when your gentleman's gentleman went to work for Mrs. Moseley at Moseley Mansion, Harvey. And she's been off in Europe for some time, I hear."

"That's right, Mr. Bunce," said Harvey. "She's trying to find some money in a bank over there, so she can keep Moseley Mansion and maybe open it to the public, the way the city council and Mayor Paddle want her to."

"Well, I hope P. M. Heister doesn't get the mayor's ear on that grand old house, too, or it might not be standing when she gets back!"

"If he tries to do anything," Harvey said, bristling, "we'll get all our friends and—and *defend* it, won't we, Woody?"

"Yeah!" said Woody.

Mr. Bunce laughed. "I was only joking, boys. No need to get out the militia just yet. Now don't you two have something better to do than hang around here all day?"

"Sure, Mr. Bunce," said Woody. "We're going over to Uncle Doody's for our free Doobie sandwich. He promised everyone on the Doody's Doobies soccer team a free Doobie this Saturday because we won our first game from the Dolly's Tamales last week."

"Congratulations!" said Mr. Bunce. "I heard about that."

"Gee, just think, Woody!" exclaimed Harvey. "A free Doobie and free bubble gum from Charlie —I mean, Sharles—all in one day!"

"Well," said Mr. Bunce, "never let it be said that Bunce's Pet Shop was outdone by Doody's Doobies or Sharles the hair stylist. So to make your day even better, grab a handful of those free brochures over there on the counter. Some outfit up North that sells chicken feed keeps sending them to me by the gross, even though I've never stocked a chicken here from the day the store opened. They've even sent me a big, free sack of chicken feed that's taking up valuable space in my storeroom."

"Gee, thanks, Mr. Bunce!" said Harvey and Woody.

"Don't mention it! Say hello to Doody for me. I only hope his place is still standing when you get there." Mr. Bunce shook his head.

"What do you mean, Mr. Bunce?" Harvey asked.

"Oh, nothing," said Mr. Bunce. "Now, pat the puppies on the head, and scoot."

"Thanks again for the free brochures, Mr. Bunce!" said Harvey.

"Yeah, thanks!" echoed Woody.

"Wow!" Harvey whispered as they left the store. "Look how many we got, Woody."

"Yeah!" said Woody happily.

Neither Harvey nor Woody had any more thought of chicken ownership than did Mr. Bunce. But, after all, when it came to free things, twenty-five was better than ten, even if it was twenty-five useless brochures advertising chicken feed!

II

Troubles

Just as Harvey and Woody stepped out the
door of Bunce's Pet Store, a bright flash nearly
blinded them. When Harvey had finished rubbing
his eyes, he was just in time to catch a glimpse of
someone ducking around the corner of the building. But he recognized the red curls on the head of
the disappearing party.

"Charlotte Grassman!" he said disgustedly.

"What was she doing?" Woody asked.

"Taking a picture of us, I guess," replied
Harvey.

Woody's eyebrows shot up. "Are we famous now or something, Harvey?"

"Woody," said Harvey in a resigned voice, "Charlotte just took our picture because she happened to get a new camera for her birthday. She never even wanted one until her little brother took that picture of us getting caught climbing the Moseley Mansion fence that time, and it got in 'Chuckle for the Day' in the *Gazette.*"

"What's so funny about us walking out of Bunce's Pet Store with a bunch of free brochures telling about chicken feed?" asked Woody.

"Nothing," said Harvey.

"Maybe it's our haircuts from Sharles the hair stylist," suggested Woody.

"I don't think so," said Harvey. "I think she just hopes we'll do something funny again, and she isn't going to take any chances on missing it. But we'll show her. We won't do anything funny for her and her old camera."

"Yeah!" said Woody.

Trying to escape the lurking Charlotte, the boys began to double-step in the direction of the small white frame house in the center of town that served as both a home and a place of business for Uncle Doody, Aunt Bird, and the Doobie sandwiches that Uncle Doody had recently invented.

"What do you suppose Mr. Bunce meant about

Uncle Doody's house still standing?'' asked Woody, catching his breath. "It looks okay to me."

"Me too," said Harvey. "Maybe Uncle Doody and Aunt Bird are thinking about moving and are going to sell their house. Maybe they want to move into a big mansion now that Uncle Doody has made all that money selling the recipe for his secret Doobie sauce."

Woody's head whipped around. "Boy, Harvey, maybe they might even leave town! Then our soccer team wouldn't have a sponsor anymore. We'd be right back where we started."

"Yeah, except that we're a lot better now that Hawkins is our coach," Harvey said. "Imagine us beating the Dolly's Tamales!"

"Yeah!" said Woody.

"But I still wouldn't want Uncle Doody to leave. I like being the Doody's Doobies."

"Me too," said Woody.

By this time the boys had arrived at the steps of the little house with the sign beside the door that read: "Doody's Doobies. Enter for the biggest treat of your life!" Harvey and Woody entered.

The small room was empty. There were no people at the four white tables with the green checked tablecloths, and no one was behind the sandwich counter, either.

23

"I wonder if anyone's been here yet for their free Doobies," Harvey said.

A head shot up from behind the counter. "Me!"

The head belonged to Pinky Patterson. Although Harvey, Woody, and lots of their friends had called Doody and Bird Patterson "Uncle Doody" and "Aunt Bird" for as long as they could remember, Pinky was the only one who could rightfully call them that. He was always hanging around the little white house.

"Where's Uncle Doody?" asked Harvey.

"He and Aunt Bird aren't packing to leave, are they?" Woody asked anxiously.

"Packing to leave?" Pinky looked at them as if he thought Woody had lost his whole mind. "He's just out back with Aunt Bird, bringing in some stuff from the freezer. Hey, Uncle Doody!" he shouted. "Two customers are here for their free Doobies!"

In a moment, Uncle Doody and Aunt Bird appeared. She was wearing the same old work jeans, and he was wiping his hands on the same old flowered apron that drooped around his knees. Neither looked one bit as if they had just made piles of money selling a secret recipe.

"Uncle Doody," Pinky said, "Woody wanted to know if you and Aunt Bird were packing to leave."

Uncle Doody laughed. "Now where did you get an idea like that, Woody?"

"Woody and I were just at Bunce's Pet Store," Harvey broke in. "Mr. Bunce said he hoped your place was still standing when we got here, Uncle Doody, so we thought maybe you and Aunt Bird had sold it and were moving away."

"Moving away?" Uncle Doody looked at Aunt Bird. "Boys, Aunt Bird and I have lived in this little house ever since it was first built, watching the town grow up around us, and this is where we plan to stay."

"Exactly!" said Aunt Bird.

"Whew!" breathed Harvey. "That's a relief."

"Yeah!" said Woody.

"You know," said Uncle Doody, handing Harvey and Woody their Doobies, "I expect what Mr. Bunce was referring to was a visitation we had the other day from Mayor Paddle and that—that Mr. P. M. Heister who's been trailing around with him lately, sticking to him like glue."

"That's right!" Aunt Bird chimed in. "They were here, all right, with Mr. Heister pretending to be all interested in Doody's new Doobie business. He was ooh-ing and ah-ing over the secret sauce in the sandwich, and all the time snooping and snuffling around like a bird dog, just trying to find one good

25

reason he can move us out of this house and tear it down."

"Now, Bird," said Uncle Doody. "Maybe we're getting too excited. We don't know anything for certain."

"*I* know it!" said Aunt Bird. "Then they were just back in here again, doing the same thing. Don't tell *me* about that Mr. What's-His-Initials Heister!"

"Could they—could they move you out?" asked Pinky, whose eyes had grown wider and wider.

"I don't see how," replied Uncle Doody, shaking his head.

"But you can be sure he's going to try, Pinky," said Aunt Bird crisply. "I'll bet he's going to be poring over those books in City Hall until the wee hours, just trying to find something he can catch us on."

Uncle Doody sighed. "Has your former gentleman's gentleman met this individual yet, Harvey? I understand Heister is some kind of distant relative of Mrs. Moseley's."

"Hawkins hasn't said anything about it, Uncle Doody," replied Harvey.

"Well, I just hope Mrs. Moseley gets back soon to protect that beautiful historical home before Mr. Initials Heister decides it ought to go, too. Modern, humph!" snorted Aunt Bird.

Woody looked at Harvey. "Mr. Bunce said something like that, too, only he said he was just joking, Aunt Bird."

"Maybe he was, but maybe he wasn't," Uncle Doody broke in. "I must admit that Mr. Heister has us all a little worried. Mayor Paddle seems to have changed all of a sudden. He's not the same man he was just a couple of weeks ago. Confound it! We've been electing him every four years for the past twenty. What's he have to go and get a new 'assistant and campaign manager' for? We liked him the way he was."

"No fool like an old fool!" announced Aunt Bird. "If he's not careful, somebody might decide to run against him."

"Well, let's talk about pleasanter things," said Uncle Doody. "I've got a present for the coach of my Doody's Doobies soccer team, Harvey. Are you going to be seeing him any time today?"

"A present for Hawkins? Wow!" said Harvey. "Sure, Uncle Doody. Woody and I were going to stop by Moseley Mansion on the way home to tell him about a change in our soccer schedule."

"Good! Then you can give him these." Uncle Doody brought out a brown paper sack from the refrigerator behind the sandwich counter. "Just be very, *very* careful, because what's inside is very, *very* breakable."

27

"What is inside?" asked Harvey.

"Eggs," replied Uncle Doody.

Woody's jaw fell. "Eggs? I thought eggs always came in a box."

"The only thing eggs *always* come in is a chicken," said Uncle Doody. "Or some other kind of bird or animal. After that, eggs go into whatever's handy, and in this case it was the paper sack my Cousin Theodore had left on the kitchen counter. These eggs are fresh in from the country!"

"We thought Hawkins ought to have them," said Aunt Bird. "Poor man, rattling around all alone in that big house! Probably not feeding himself too well, with Mrs. Moseley gone. These fresh brown eggs will do him good."

"Boy, he'll be glad!" said Harvey. "Thanks!"

"Don't mention it," said Uncle Doody. "But come to think of it, we've got something here for each of you three boys. Bird, where'd we put those raffle tickets Theodore brought us?"

"They're on the counter, right there under your nose, Doody," replied Aunt Bird.

"Oh!" said Uncle Doody, looking sheepish. "Well, so happens Theodore and Mildred bought a whole handful of these raffle tickets for their church picnic. He brought us four, so here's one for each of you."

"Boy, free tickets!" exclaimed Harvey. "Gee, thanks, Uncle Doody! Maybe if I win, it'll be something I can keep. Woody and I were just guessing the marbles in the jar in Mr. Bunce's window to win a puppy, but if I won I couldn't keep the puppy anyway, because Betsy has allergies."

"Well, I don't think the prizes for this raffle will include anything as exciting as a puppy, Harvey," said Uncle Doody. "It would probably be one of Mildred's famous spice cakes, or somebody else's famous strawberry preserves, but at least it would be something you could keep or use. Anyway, you're pretty good at winning contests, so maybe you'll be lucky this time, too"

"What if we win?" Woody asked, looking anxious. "Will somebody bring us our prizes?"

Uncle Doody laughed. "Don't worry, Woody. If you win, you'll get your prize!"

Free bubble gum! A contest for a free puppy! Free brochures advertising chicken feed! Free Doobies! And now free raffle tickets!

"Wow!" said Harvey to Woody as they were leaving the little white frame house. "I can't even count how many free things we got today."

"Yeah!" said Woody. "Me neither."

"You take good care of those eggs, Harvey

Small!" Aunt Bird called to him from the porch.

"I will, Aunt Bird!" Harvey yelled back. "Boy!" he said to Woody. "We even got free eggs for Hawkins!"

"Yeah!" said Woody.

III

Splat!

"Well, Harvey, at least we lost Charlotte," Woody said. "I don't see her anywhere."

"We didn't see her before either, Woody," Harvey replied, "and she was there anyway. We'd just better not do anything dumb."

"We won't! We won't!" said Woody. "Hey, Harvey, look!" he shouted suddenly.

"Don't scare me like that!" said Harvey. "I just about dropped Hawkins' eggs. Boy oh boy, Woody, if you'd made me do that . . . !"

"Okay, then—look, Harvey," said Woody,

dropping his voice to a ridiculous whisper. "There's Mayor Paddle and that Mr. Heister over by that lamppost near the Regal Theater. What's Mr. Heister doing, staring up at the light bulb and waving his arms around? That looks weird!"

"Yeah, it sure does," said Harvey.

"Maybe they just came out from seeing *Fango and the Space Patrol* at the Regal, and Mr. Heister thinks he's a space pilot," said Woody.

"Or maybe he's telling Mayor Paddle ways you can modernize a lamppost," said Harvey.

"How *do* you modernize a lamppost?" asked Woody.

"I don't know. Maybe the same way you modernize a puppy."

"Hch, heh, heh! Very funny, Harvey."

A few curious onlookers had gathered around Mayor Paddle and Mr. Heister, and Harvey and Woody joined them. What was happening there sounded pretty boring, though. Mr. Heister kept talking in a loud voice, as if he wanted everyone to hear his ideas about beauty going hand in hand with modernization. And he explained how that could even apply to lampposts. Mayor Paddle, meanwhile, looked as if the lamppost they were discussing was not the thing nearest and dearest to his heart and he really wished he were someplace else. Harvey and Woody, fortunately, could not only *wish* they were someplace else, they could do something about it.

"Ho-hum," said Harvey.

"Yeah," agreed Woody. "Let's leave."

They broke away from the group, but as they did, Harvey saw something that made him clutch his egg sack tighter. "Uh-oh, Woody, looks like the kiddy matinee is just letting out. There's Mrs. Jones and Pee Wee, getting his new birthday bike from the stand. It looks like a big crowd, and I sure don't want anyone bumping into me while I've got these eggs. Come on, let's cross the street!"

"Gee, Harvey, I'm too tired to cross the street," said Woody.

"Then you'd better hold my chicken-feed brochures so I can protect my eggs," said Harvey.

Woody grabbed the brochures and jumped in front of Harvey, flailing his arms. "*I'll* protect you, Harvey. Hey, I'm Fango, the space patrol pilot. Whoosh! Whoosh!"

"Hi, Harvey and Woody!" several of their friends called out as they brushed past. It didn't seem to worry anybody that Woody was jumping around on the sidewalk and waving his arms like a lunatic. Harvey decided Woody's idea was pretty good, and that he and the eggs would make it through safely.

"Hi, Mayor Paddle!" sang out most of the boys and girls.

Mayor Paddle had known a lot of them since they were born. He seemed relieved to be excused from the important duty of studying the lamppost and happily began patting little heads. Mr. Heister, however, looked as if he had just eaten something that gave him indigestion. Children clearly did not agree with him.

Meanwhile, back at the bicycle rack, Pee Wee had finally succeeded in mounting his little bike. As his mother watched him anxiously, he made a shaky start onto the sidewalk. By now the space between the theater and Harvey and Woody was fairly well cleared, and he finally caught sight of them.

"Hey, look at me now, Harvey and Woody!" he shouted. "No more training wheels!" With a happy smile on his face, Pee Wee began to wobble right toward the two boys.

"Pee Wee!" shrieked Mrs. Jones. "You come back here right this instant!"

But Pee Wee was much too excited about his new achievement to worry about anything his mother might have to say. He teetered on toward Harvey and Woody.

"Pee Wee, stop!" they hollered.

"I can't!" cried Pee Wee. "I don't know how!" He had begun to look scared.

"We'll get him, Mrs. Jones!" yelled Harvey. Holding the sack of eggs away from himself with an outstretched arm, he stationed himself next to Woody. "You get one handlebar, and I'll get the other."

"Right!" said Woody.

But unfortunately, with a thoroughly frightened Pee Wee at the helm, the bicycle had a mind of its own. Suddenly it decided to wobble to the other side of Harvey, where a convenient brown paper sack hung right there for Pee Wee to grab like a brass ring on a merry-go-round. So Pee Wee grabbed.

SPLAT!

SPLAT!

SPLAT!

Eggs burst on the sidewalk like miniature yellow bombs. But Harvey and Woody were too intent on capturing Pee Wee to worry about the lost eggs. They took out after him, only to come thumping down on their rear ends as their feet skidded on the slippery eggs. Chicken-feed brochures, freed from Woody's hands, rained down around them.

Pee Wee, however, finally came to a stop, anyway.

"Ooof!" cried Mayor Paddle as the bicycle

crashed right into his generous stomach, knocking him right down on *his* rear end. "Ouch!" said Mayor Paddle. "Little boy, are you all right?" he asked anxiously. "Oh, it's you, Pee Wee. Didn't hurt yourself, did you?"

Pee Wee shook his head and grinned. By rights, he should have been howling his head off, except that he had just had an exciting adventure, having knocked down three people, while he himself was still seated on his bicycle!

"Come, come, Your Honor, try to get up!" Mr. Heister frantically tried to pull the mayor up. "Your image! We must think about your image!"

Huffing and puffing, Mayor Paddle tried unsuccessfully to hoist himself to his feet. "It's not my image that's troubling me right now!" he moaned, rubbing his behind in a most undignified manner.

And just then there was a bright flash, which Mr. Heister recognized at once. "Who took that picture? Little girl, did you take a picture?"

"Oh, yes!" said Charlotte primly. "My mother's a reporter on the *Gazette,* and I'm going to see that this gets into 'Chuckle for the Day'!"

"A picture of the mayor in 'Chuckle for the Day'?" said Mr. Heister in a horrified voice.

"Oh, no!" said Charlotte. "This picture is of Harvey Small and Woody Woodruff, sitting in the middle of all those busted eggs. I knew if I hung around them long enough, I'd get a good picture. I'm going to get more, too. My little brother just got *one* picture of them in 'Chuckle for the Day.' *I'm* going to get a *lot!*"

"Oh murder, Woody, we did it again!" moaned Harvey.

"Yeah!" said Woody.

Mr. Heister simply mopped his relieved brow with a huge silk handkerchief monogrammed "PM" in big, important, red letters.

IV

Dreadful News

Harvey decided that every time he walked through the tall, iron gates and up the long walk to Moseley Mansion, he would get a strange feeling in the middle of his stomach. The house was so huge, so gray and shadowy even in the bright sunlight. When even the tiniest breeze ruffled through the thick ivy that covered the walls, the leaves shivered and whispered as if a ghost were passing by.

Harvey couldn't help remembering the time he and Hawkins had gone on a ghost hunt when Moseley Mansion was supposed to be deserted, only to discover that the ghost was Mrs. Moseley. She had returned from her travels abroad and was prowling the halls with a flickering candle because the electricity had not been turned back on yet. That was how Mrs. Moseley came to meet Hawkins, and how he came to work for her. But Harvey was certain a ghost still wandered the halls of Moseley Mansion. It looked particularly dismal and deserted today, and he wished Woody could have come with him. But they had lost so much time sliding around on eggs that Woody had to race to his dentist's appointment, and now Harvey was alone.

Because he was visiting Hawkins, and not Mrs. Moseley, Harvey went directly around to the back door and pressed the bell. The usually cheerful buzz from inside seemed to have a lonely, hollow sound today. Where was Hawkins, anyway? Harvey waited and waited and then pressed the button again. Finally, he heard footsteps, and the door opened.

Despite the fact that Harvey and his former gentleman's gentleman were the best of friends, Harvey was startled each time Hawkins arrived at the door in his striped trousers, the long-tailed black jacket, and gray silk tie with a stickpin in it. Nor could Harvey ever get used to the very proper, stiff-as-old-glue expression Hawkins wore. Today it seemed even stiffer, and mournful, too. At least until he recognized the visitor as being Harvey.

"Oh sir, how splendid to see you! I'm so sorry I kept you waiting, but I was in the drawing room laying sheets over the furniture. It took me a moment longer to arrive."

"That's okay, Hawkins," said Harvey. "I'm just glad you were here."

"Won't you step in, sir?"

Harvey stepped in and followed Hawkins into the bright, cheery kitchen. The awesome rooms in the rest of Moseley Mansion scared him a little, but one room Harvey did like was the huge kitchen, with the tall, white cupboards and blue and white Dutch tiles around the counters. The kitchen was so big a person could practically roller-skate in it.

"Hawkins?" said Harvey.

"Sir?"

"Why were you laying sheets over the furniture? Are you going to be painting or something?" Harvey asked. "Can I help?"

"Thank you so much, sir, but it's nothing like that. The sheets are because—oh dear, sir, I suppose I must tell you the dreadful news." Hawkins' long face seemed to grow even longer.

"Dreadful news?"

"Most dreadful, sir!"

"Gee, Hawkins, what is it?"

"Well, sir, perhaps you would care to seat yourself at the table while I relate it all to you."

"I'd care to, Hawkins—but, oh boy, I can't do that," Harvey added quickly. "I'm a mess."

"A mess, sir? Admittedly you are not attired in coat and tie, or your soccer costume, but your—er—daily attire of corduroy trousers and—ah—sweatshirt is quite appropriate for—"

Before Hawkins could finish, Harvey turned slowly around so his back was facing his former gentleman's gentleman.

"Oh my word, sir!"

Harvey sighed. "That's what I meant, Hawkins—*eggs!*"

"Eggs, sir?"

"Woody says I look like an omelet," said Harvey. "He looks like one too, Hawkins."

"But I don't understand, sir. How did you and Mr. Woodruff come to be looking like—ah—omelets?"

"It was an accident," said Harvey.

"I suspected as much, sir. I do hope you and Mr. Woodruff were in no way hurt in this mishap."

"Just our bottoms," said Harvey. "But we're okay, Hawkins. I wouldn't have come with eggs all over my rear, except they were a present to you from Uncle Doody and Aunt Bird, and I thought you ought to see them. Well, what's left of them, anyway."

"That is very kind of you, sir. And how very kind of *them* to think of me!"

"They were fresh brown eggs right from Uncle Doody's Cousin Theodore's farm," Harvey said. "Aunt Bird thought you probably aren't eating properly with Mrs. Moseley away, and she said these would do you good, Hawkins."

"Fresh brown eggs from the country! Oh, sir, what memories that conjures! You know, when I was a lad, I often visited my grandmother in the country," Hawkins said in a faraway voice. "Plump strawberries, clotted cream, and fresh brown eggs warm from the hen's nest. Oh, it was simply splendid, sir!"

"I—I'm really sorry about busting the eggs, Hawkins," said Harvey in a small voice.

"Oh, sir!" Hawkins said, collecting himself. "It is I who should be sorry, causing you to feel worse than you already do. Eggs are only eggs, after all. It is the thought that matters, and *that* was delivered to me quite whole."

"It—it really was an accident, Hawkins."

"Of course it was, sir!" said Hawkins. "Would you care to tell me how the mishap occurred, and how the eggs came to be—er—busted?"

"Well," said Harvey, "Woody and I were walking down Main Street just as the kiddy matinee was letting out. They're playing *Fango and the Space Patrol*. Everyone says it's a neat movie, Hawkins. Would you like to go with Woody and me to see it sometime?"

"*Fango and the Space Patrol?*" said Hawkins weakly. "That—that would be splendid, sir. Now, as you were saying about the mishap?"

"Oh yeah," said Harvey. "Well, one of the kids coming out of the movie was Pee Wee Jones, with his mother. And Pee Wee wanted to show off to Woody and me how he could ride his new bicycle without training wheels. The only thing was, he didn't know how to stop. Woody and I tried to stop him, but we missed, and Pee Wee grabbed at me and got my sack of eggs instead."

"I believe I see the unfortunate picture, sir," said Hawkins. "The eggs fell from the sack, and when you and Mr. Woodruff attempted to retrieve Master Pee Wee, you slipped on the eggs, thus ending up looking like—ah—omelets."

"That's exactly what happened," said Harvey.

"But what befell Master Pee Wee, sir? Is he now safe and sound?"

"Oh, he's okay, Hawkins, but he ran right into Mayor Paddle before he stopped, and knocked the mayor over on *his* rear end," said Harvey.

"Oh dear, sir!"

"Well," said Harvey, "at least it wasn't Mayor Paddle that got his picture taken by that nosy Charlotte Grassman and her new camera. It was *us*, Hawkins. So it looks like Woody and I are going to be in 'Chuckle for the Day'!"

"Oh no, not again, sir!"

Harvey nodded. "Boy, that Mr. Heister sure was glad it was us getting our picture in 'Chuckle for the Day,' and not Mayor Paddle!"

Hawkins' long, thin face had suddenly grown pale. "Mr.—Mr. Heister, sir?"

"Is something wrong, Hawkins?" Harvey asked quickly. "Do you know him?"

"I have made his acquaintance, sir," replied Hawkins stiffly.

"Hawkins!" Harvey exclaimed. "Does—does he have anything to do with that—that dreadful news you were going to tell me about?"

"In a roundabout manner, there is a connection, sir."

"Can you tell me about it now?" asked Harvey.

"Most assuredly, sir. But I insist that you be seated. Eggs on a kitchen chair are of no consequence. May I serve you a glass of milk and some—some bread and margarine?"

Bread and margarine? Harvey was used to having delicious cookies or a big slice of cake whenever he visited Hawkins at Moseley Mansion. But bread and margarine? "I—I guess so."

"I must offer my apologies, sir," Hawkins said, "but I—I have not been to the grocer's today."

From the view inside the Moseley Mansion refrigerator, it looked as if Hawkins hadn't been to the grocer's in a month! The refrigerator was practically empty. The last time Harvey had been there, it was bulging with food. What could have happened since then? Hawkins was clearly embarrassed, however, so Harvey decided he wouldn't say anything.

"Have you perhaps noticed, sir," said Hawkins as he poured Harvey's milk, "that I have not been quite myself at our last soccer practices?"

Harvey thought a moment. Now that Hawkins mentioned it, Harvey remembered that he *had* noticed it. "I guess I did, Hawkins. I thought maybe you were tired or something, looking after this big old house while Mrs. Moseley was away. I was wondering if all us Doody's Doobies should offer to help."

"How very kind of you, sir! But I was not in fact tired, only troubled. You see, Mrs. Moseley had written me that she was unwell, and following that time, I had no communication from her at all. Needless to say, sir, I was deeply concerned."

"I'll bet you were, Hawkins."

"In any event, sir," continued Hawkins, "the next communication I had was in the form of a visit from Mr. Heister."

"Uh-oh!" said Harvey.

"Precisely so, sir," said Hawkins. "The visit was not of the most—*cordial* variety. Mr. Heister delivered the terrible news that—that Mrs. Moseley is very, very ill. She is so ill, in fact, that the people with whom she is residing in Europe wrote her old friend Mayor Paddle, asking that he appoint someone to take charge of her affairs here until she recovers. Since Mr. Heister is related to Mrs. Moseley, even though quite distantly, Mayor Paddle decided he would be the ideal choice. From now on, all my communication with Mrs. Moseley must be through Mr. Heister, I am informed."

"Oh no!" groaned Harvey.

"Quite so, sir!" said Hawkins. "And Mr. Heister has also informed me that I can no longer continue coaching the Doody's Doobies."

"Oh no!" moaned Harvey.

"Please don't be distressed about this, sir. I have already spoken with Mr. Hicks, your league chairman, and he assures me that you have become such a fine soccer team that he will have people clamoring to be your coach."

"Boy, thanks to you Hawkins!" said Harvey.

"But the Doody's Doobies sure aren't going to like it."

"And I shall miss coaching them, sir."

"Why won't Mr. Heister let you coach us anymore?" Harvey asked.

"He seems to feel, sir, that I am being paid to care for Moseley Mansion, not a—a—oh dear, sir—a bunch of brats! But the fact is that he has also informed me that the funds Mrs. Moseley had hoped to recover in the bank in Europe were not there. Therefore, I shall be receiving little or no pay for my services."

"That's terrible, Hawkins!" Harvey thought of the empty refrigerator. Why, Hawkins was probably *living* on bread and margarine!

"It does not present the most cheerful outlook, sir. But the truth of this whole matter is that I suspect Mr. Heister wishes me to *leave* Moseley Mansion!"

"Did he say that?" asked Harvey.

"Not in so many words, sir. But he suggested that if I did not care for the—ah—new arrangements, perhaps I might be happier taking my services elsewhere."

Harvey gasped. "Are you going to, Hawkins?"

"Most assuredly not, sir! I am quite persuaded that there is skulduggery afoot, and that someone wishes a clear field in which to carry on his underhanded deeds. I intend to stay right here and care for Moseley Mansion until I hear from Mrs. Moseley herself that my services are not required. And I shall also attempt to find out what is at the bottom of Mr. P. M. Heister's great anxiety to see the last of me."

"But—but what about not getting any pay, Hawkins? How are you going—to eat?" Harvey was really worried.

"Oh, you must not concern yourself, sir. I have a bit of money put away, and I shall make it stretch as far as possible."

"Can't anybody help?" Harvey asked. "I'll bet all the Doody's Doobies would like to—"

"Oh no, sir!" Hawkins broke in. "Absolutely not! It's a matter of a—"

"I know," said Harvey, "a gentleman's gentleman's pride. I remember all about that."

"Quite right, sir. So think no more about it."

"We-e-ell," said Harvey, "if you *do* need anything . . . "

"I shall let you know at once, sir," said Hawkins. "That is a gentleman's gentleman's promise."

V

Guess What, Harvey?

There it was, right on the class bulletin board—that morning's "Chuckle for the Day" from the *Gazette*. Charlotte was so proud of her picture, she wanted the whole class, not to mention the whole world, to see it. Practically everyone in the room was clustered around the board looking at the picture, except Harvey and Woody. They had seen as much of it as they wanted, over their respective breakfast tables that morning.

Charlotte was reading the caption under the picture, for about the tenth time, to anyone who cared to hear it.

"Eggstra—eggstra!" read Charlotte. "Two boys who seem to appear in this column on a regular basis, appear again this week, swimming in a sea of eggs. Harvey Small and Woody Woodruff, while attempting to rescue young Pee Wee Jones and his runaway bicycle, somehow managed to let slide through their fingers not only Pee Wee, but a sack of eggs as well. The eggs dropped to the sidewalk, and the boys dropped on the eggs. It was a very eggsciting scene—no yolking, folks! The hero of the hour was our own Mayor Paddle, who stopped the bicycle and delivered Pee Wee safely to his mother. The above picture, incidentally, was taken by fifth-grader Charlotte Grassman, who is none other than the daughter of Sandra Grassman, ace *Gazette* reporter. Keep 'em coming, Charlotte!"

Slouching down in his seat, as far as he could, Harvey dug his fist into his chin. "Oh brother!"

"Yeah, you said it, Harvey!" replied Woody.

Their friends Pinky Patterson, David Warhurst, Eddy Platt, and Irving Weiner, who had all heard Charlotte give an earlier reading, came over and dropped into the desks around Harvey and Woody.

"Gee, I wish I could have *my* picture in 'Chuckle for the Day'!" Irving said.

"Me too!" said Eddy.

"Boy, you don't know what you're saying,"

51

Harvey told them. "You don't get your picture there because you're some handsome TV star. You get there because you did something really stupid."

"Yeah," said Woody. "And we did!"

"It wasn't *your* fault," Pinky said.

"Charlotte doesn't care *whose* fault anything is." Harvey bit gloomily into the rubber tip of his yellow pencil.

"That's right," Woody agreed. "And she's going to keep following us around until we do something else stupid. She figures we're her best chance of getting another picture into 'Chuckle for the Day.' "

"Maybe you'll accidentally do something heroic and famous, like Mayor Paddle did, and she'll get a picture of that," said David.

"We'll never do anything heroic *or* famous," said Harvey. He spit out the rubber tip he had accidentally bitten off. "Anyway, Mayor Paddle didn't do anything so heroic. Pee Wee ran right into him and knocked him over, and that's how the bicycle stopped."

"How come Charlotte didn't take a picture of that?" asked Irving.

"Because she was too busy taking a picture of us, dopey," replied Woody.

"Well then," said David, "how come the paper called Mayor Paddle a hero?"

Harvey looked at Woody and shrugged. *"We* don't know, but I'll bet that Mr. Heister had something to do with it. I'll bet he made up the whole story and got someone on the paper to print it that way."

"Who's Mr. Heister?" Eddy asked.

"He's Mayor Paddle's new assistant, and he's going to help him in the campaign," Pinky said.

"Is Mayor Paddle going to campaign this year?" asked Irving. "What for?"

"Uncle Doody and Aunt Bird think Mr. Heister talked the mayor into it," Pinky replied. "They sure don't like all the stuff he's been doing one bit."

"There's some stuff they don't even know about too," said Harvey. "I guess it's all right for me to say because you'll all find out this afternoon, anyway, but Mr. Heister told Hawkins he can't be our soccer coach anymore!"

"Can't be our soccer coach!" Irving exploded. "How come he can tell Hawkins that?"

Harvey exchanged glances with Woody, who knew the whole story. "He can because Mrs. Moseley is sick, and Mr. Heister is looking after Moseley Mansion and all that. That's how come, Irving!"

"Oh no!" Pinky, Eddy, David, and Irving all groaned.

"Tell them the other stuff about Hawkins, too, Harvey," Woody said.

Harvey cast a glance over his shoulder. He didn't think the stuff Hawkins had told him should travel very far, and Harvey knew he had to be careful, with Charlotte Grassman's big eyes and ears in the room. But the school bell rang just then, anyway.

"Look, everyone," Irving whispered. "Let's all meet at my house after soccer practice. Then Harvey can tell us the other stuff about Hawkins. Is that okay?"

They all nodded that it was okay.

"Class, take your seats, please," said Mrs. Pettit, their fifth-grade teacher. "Charlotte, you may stop reading. I'm certain the whole class now knows everything it needs to know about 'Chuckle for the Day.' Woody?"

"Yes, Mrs. Pettit," said Woody earnestly.

Woody's earnestness didn't do any good. "You may bring Lollypop up to my desk, Woody, where he will reside in a locked drawer until the end of the school day." It always surprised everyone, especially Woody, that Mrs. Pettit could see things going on when she never seemed even to pay any attention to them. That included Woody's pet garter snake, Lollypop, which he frequently brought to school.

"Gee, Mrs. Pettit, he'll suffocate," said Woody.

"He has never suffocated in that drawer before," said Mrs. Pettit, "and I'm certain he won't today. Harvey?"

"Yes, Mrs. Pettit."

"Will you please try to shut that middle window a little tighter so there won't be a draft on all you children over there."

"I don't think I can," said Harvey.

"Well, try. It looks as if we probably won't be getting the new windows Mayor Paddle promised us after all, so we'll have to do the best we can with these. I'm afraid we won't be getting the new books in the library, either." Mrs. Pettit sighed. "It seems that, instead, we are going to have all our doors and window frames painted a bright orange to—to match the new paint on the city lampposts. Oh well!" she concluded dimly. "You may open up your orange—I mean, English books to page sixty-seven, please."

Harvey and Woody looked at each other with raised eyebrows. Only someone who didn't care much for children would not mind letting them freeze in the winter, or go without books, while they were trying to make a big impression by splashing doors and window sills with bright orange paint. It began to look as if Mr. P. M. Heister was not only managing Mayor Paddle's campaign and Moseley Mansion, but just about everything else in town, as well!

The boys all hurried right over to Irving's house the minute soccer practice ended. They stopped in the kitchen briefly for glasses of lemonade and then raced up to Irving's room. They had discussed their new soccer coach all the way to the house, so there wasn't much more to say about that. The new coach was okay, they all decided, but he wasn't Hawkins.

"I sure wish we still had Hawkins. No one's ever going to be the same," Pinky said when they had all distributed themselves around on Irving's bed, Irving's desk chair, and Irving's floor.

"Yeah!" everyone agreed.

"Okay, Harvey," Irving said, "now you can tell us the other stuff about Hawkins."

Harvey looked carefully around the room to make sure that just Irving, Pinky, David, Eddy, and Woody were there. He didn't trust that Charlotte Grassman for one minute, even up in Irving's room, and now he was getting the feeling that Mr Heister just might be lurking about, too.

"You all remember, don't you," began Harvey, "that Mrs. Moseley was going to see if that bank in

Europe had enough for her to keep Moseley Mansion *and* Hawkins?"

Everyone nodded. They all remembered that.

"Well, Mr. Heister said there wasn't *any* money, so that means Hawkins is only going to get paid a little bit, or maybe not get paid at all."

"Nothing at all!" exclaimed Eddy. "Does that mean Hawkins is going to leave, Harvey?"

"Nope!" Harvey canvassed the room again, and dropped his voice to a whisper. "Hawkins thinks there's something weird going on, and that Mr. Heister *wants* him to leave."

"But he told Harvey he's not going to!" said Woody.

"Wow!" breathed Irving, Pinky, Eddy, and David. Their eyes were practically popping out of their heads.

"I don't understand," said Pinky. "If Hawkins doesn't have any money, how's he going to live?"

"He says he has a little money saved up," Harvey replied. "But I don't think he has very much. You ought to see the inside of his refrigerator. There's just a big bunch of nothing in there."

"Boy!" said David. "Do you think he's going to starve to death, Harvey?"

"I hope not," said Harvey, "but I don't know what to do about it."

"Maybe *we* could earn some money and give it to Hawkins!" Pinky said excitedly.

"Gee, Pinky, you know how good *we* are at earning money. If Hawkins was counting on us, he'd *really* starve to death!" Harvey said. "Besides, he wouldn't take money from us, anyway. You remember I told you that gentleman's gentleman's pride stuff."

"Yeah, that's right," said Pinky.

"How about thinking of a way for Hawkins to earn money for himself?" Irving suggested.

"Hey, that's neat, Irving!" Harvey said. "Do you have any ideas?"

"Well, every time my mom has a tea, I could ask her to hire Hawkins."

"Does your mom have a lot of teas?" asked Harvey.

Irving thought a moment. "I guess she's never had one."

"That's about when mine had one," said Woody. "Never!"

Nobody else could remember his mother having a tea either. It looked as if Hawkins would still starve to death if he had to depend on the mothers' tea business.

"Hawkins could have my paper route, Harvey," said Pinky.

"That's nice, Pinky," Harvey said. "But I don't

think a gentleman's gentleman does that kind of stuff. Besides, you couldn't miss Hawkins if he was riding around on a bicycle delivering papers, and I don't think he ought to do anything Mr. Heister might find out about. He says Hawkins is being paid just to take care of Moseley Mansion. That's why he can't coach the Doody's Doobies anymore."

"But Hawkins isn't being paid *anything!*" exclaimed David.

"I know," said Harvey glumly. "But at least he gets to stay at Moseley Mansion so he can find out what's going on."

"Yeah, that's right!" everyone agreed.

"We'll just have to think of something Hawkins can do that Mr. Heister can't find out about," said Harvey.

"Yeah!" agreed everyone.

They were all thinking so hard, trying to come up with ideas, that no one even heard the telephone ring. Then Mrs. Weiner called up the stairs. "Harvey, you're wanted on the telephone. It's your sister, Betsy."

Betsy calling Harvey on the telephone? What did *she* want? Gee, she was interrupting his important conference with the boys. How did she even know he was at Irving's house?

Harvey picked up the phone. "Hello."

"Guess what, Harvey?" said Betsy. "Ah—choo!" Betsy sneezed right into the receiver.

"How did you know where I was?" asked Harvey.

"Mommy and Daddy told me I was to call everywhere until I found you," reported Betsy. "Ah—ah—choo!"

"Well, it better be important," said Harvey.

"It is," said Betsy primly. "Guess what, Harvey?"

"I'm not going to guess anything," replied Harvey crossly.

"That's all right," said Betsy, "because I wouldn't tell you anyway. But you're supposed to come right home."

"I'm not coming home just because you say so."

"Mother!" yelled Betsy. "Harvey says he won't come. Ah—ah—ah—choo!"

"Harvey?" This next voice on the telephone belonged to Harvey's mother. "You start home right away, please!"

"Gee, Mom," said Harvey, "I'm doing some important stuff over at Irving's house."

"Well," replied his mother, "you have some important stuff to do over at your own house. So you start home right this minute."

"Ah—ah—choo!" sneezed poor Betsy in the background.

"Right this minute, Harvey!" repeated Harvey's mother.

Harvey guessed from the tone of his mother's voice that that was exactly what he had better do.

VI

Ah—Choo!

Harvey raced all the way home from Irving's house, wondering what was so important. Just being late for dinner wouldn't have done it, and he wasn't late, anyway. Had he done something terrible he didn't remember? Harvey tried remembering all the terrible things he had done that day.

He had thrown his bedspread up over his bed without making it up underneath. He had squeezed the toothpaste tube too hard and squirted toothpaste all over the mirror while making faces at himself. Then he had forgotten to brush his teeth, but had left the toothpaste all over the mirror. Finally, he had been tinkering before breakfast with the spring of the old flashlight from his free-thing collection, and busted it.

But not making a bed, or failing to clean up squirted toothpaste, did not seem like major crimes to Harvey. Nobody at school had commented on how dirty his teeth looked, so that couldn't be it. As for his flashlight—well, his family considered his whole free-thing collection to be the worst kind of junk, so they ought to be happy if some of it got busted. No, something must have happened that Harvey knew nothing about.

He burst through the front door and tore into the kitchen, still peeling off his jacket. His mother, father, and Betsy were all there waiting for him.

"Ah—choo!" went Betsy, the moment Harvey appeared.

"Oh dear!" said Mrs. Small.

"Harvey," said Mr. Small sternly, "have you by any chance entered another contest lately without knowing what the prize was going to be?

"You mean like when I won a gentleman's gentleman for a whole month?" asked Harvey.

"That's exactly what I mean," replied Mr. Small. "Just like when you won Hawkins."

"Gee, Dad, that turned out okay, didn't it?"

Mr. Small looked at Mrs. Small, who simply threw up her hands and shrugged.

"Er—ah—well, yes, Harvey, but—but that's beside the point. I shall repeat my question. Have you entered another contest lately without knowing what the prize was going to be?"

"Nope," said Harvey.

"Well then, did you by any chance enter a contest in which you *knew* what the prize would be?" inquired Mr. Small.

"Yeah, I did that," said Harvey.

"Aha!" said Mr. Small triumphantly. "Would you like to tell me about it?"

"Sure, Dad," said Harvey. "I made a guess at how many marbles were in a jar in Bunce's Pet Store window. The prize is going to be a puppy."

"A puppy?" said both Mr. and Mrs. Small.

"Yeah!" said Harvey. "A neat little puppy! But Mr. Bunce knows that if I win it, I'm going to give it to Woody, and he's going to give it to Gwendolyn. Mr. Bunce knows I couldn't keep a puppy because of Betsy's allergies."

"I see," said Mr. Small limply. He looked at Mrs. Small, who once again threw up her hands and shrugged.

"Harvey, are you quite sure that's the only contest you've entered?" asked Mr. Small.

"Sure, I'm sure, Dad," said Harvey.

"Well then," said Mr. Small, drawing a deep breath, "can you please explain what twelve live chickens are doing at this moment in our backyard?"

"T-t-twelve live chickens?" stammered Harvey.

"Twelve," repeated Mr. Small firmly. "Two crates, containing six live chickens each, are at present reposing on the back lawn."

"B-b-but where did they come from?" said Harvey.

"That's what we'd like to know," replied Mr. Small.

"Betsy discovered them when she came home from school," Mrs. Small said, "and she's been sneezing her head off ever since."

"Ah—choo!" sneezed Betsy obligingly.

"How do you know the chickens are for me?" asked Harvey.

"Because you're the big enterer of contests around here, Harvey," said Mr. Small. "And there is a small card on one crate that says, 'Congratulations to the raffle winner, from Theodore and Mildred,' whoever they may be."

"Theodore and Mildred?" Harvey thought a moment and then slapped his forehead. "Theodore is Uncle Doody's cousin who lives in the country. I—I guess I won the raffle."

"But you said the puppy contest was the only one you'd entered, Harvey," said Mr. Small.

"I didn't enter this one," said Harvey. "Uncle Doody gave Woody and Pinky and me each one of the raffle tickets his cousin gave him and Aunt Bird. But they said the prizes would just be cakes or preserves or something like that. Nobody said anything about chickens. Can I go out and see them? Can I, please?" asked Harvey excitedly.

"I suppose there's no reason why you can't," said Mr. Small. "But of course you can't keep them, Harvey."

"That's right, dear," said Mrs. Small. "You'll just have to call Uncle Doody and explain to him. Perhaps he'll call his cousin and arrange to have the birds picked up. Explain that we'd like to have them removed as soon as possible."

Harvey barely heard most of this, because he was already halfway out the back door. Betsy shot out right after him.

"Betsy!" screamed Mrs. Small. "You come right back here. You know what those chicken feathers will do to you!"

But Betsy paid no attention, and so a few moments later Mr. and Mrs. Small, Harvey, *and* Betsy were all standing around the chicken crates. Betsy practically had her nose right down inside one.

"Ah—ah—ah—choo!"

"Betsy, you get right away from there!" ordered Mrs. Small. "Next thing you know, you'll be breaking out in hives."

Mr. Small bodily lifted the reluctant Betsy and set her back from the tempting crates.

"Gee, Mom and Dad!" exclaimed Harvey, "Aren't they neat! Look at that one in there. She looks like she ought to be called Lulu Belle."

"Now don't go giving names to any of those chickens, Harvey," said Mrs. Small. "It's not going to do any good. The chickens have to go, and that's that!"

"Aw gee," said Harvey. "Couldn't we keep just one?"

"Not one, Harvey," said Mr. Small.

"Hey!" Harvey blurted. "I'll bet Woody would like to have my chickens. He takes just about any free stuff I ever give him."

"I'm sure Woody would be glad to accept your chickens," said Mrs. Small. "But I'm just as sure that Mr. and Mrs. Woodruff wouldn't let him. Woody forgets to take care of his dog Blazer half the time. I just hope neither of you two boys wins Bunce's puppy either, because I'm quite certain Mrs. Woodruff will put her foot down on that as well."

"Gee, Mom," said Harvey.

"We're sorry, Harvey," said Mr. Small.

"Ah-choo!" sneezed Betsy.

That Betsy and her allergies! thought Harvey. It wasn't her fault, but he really did want to keep those chickens. He stuck a finger through the slats of one crate to pet Lulu Belle. Was that a tear he saw in one eye?

Then suddenly Harvey let out a yell. "Wow! Hey, Mom and Dad, come over here and look inside this crate. Do you see what I see?"

"Betsy, that doesn't include you," said Mrs. Small. But Betsy paid no attention and peered into the crate with her mother and father.

"Ah—ah—ah—choo!"

Mr. Small lifted her away from the crate, but returned to peer into it himself.

"Isn't that an egg?" asked Harvey excitedly.

"It certainly has the shape of one," said Mr. Small.

"And chickens do tend to lay eggs," said Mrs. Small, "though I wouldn't think a chicken would want to lay one in such—such uncomfortable quarters."

"Gee, a real egg!" breathed Harvey. "Now can we keep the chickens?"

"No," said Harvey's mother and father.

"Harvey," said Mr. Small, "our yard is simply too small. There isn't any place where you could keep a chicken coop far enough way from Betsy. If we had a very, very large yard—but then we don't, so there is no use discussing it further."

A very large yard? Harvey knew someone who had a very, very, *very* large yard. So large in fact, that it was called an estate. That was the yard surrounding Moseley Mansion!

"Mom, Dad!" Harvey blurted. "I know someone who has a very large yard, and it's far away from Betsy too. *Hawkins!*"

"No!" said Harvey's mother and father.

"Absolutely not!" said Mrs. Small. "You are not going to impose on that kind man by asking him to keep your chickens for you."

"But I have a really neat idea about it," said Harvey. "And I think you ought to *listen* to it anyway."

"Well, there's no reason we can't listen, Harvey," said Mr. Small. "But don't get your hopes up."

So Harvey presented his idea to his mother and father. When he had finished, they looked at each other with raised eyebrows.

"We-e-ell . . . " said Mrs. Small.

"I'll admit it's not the worst idea I've ever heard, Harvey," said Mr. Small.

"I thig id's a nead idea, just like Harvey says," said Betsy. "Ah—ah—ah—ah—choo!"

Harvey's eyes widened. Support from his little sister? "Gee, thanks, Betsy! So may I talk to Hawkins? May I?"

"We-e-ell . . ."

"Gee thanks, Mom and Dad!" Harvey was off like a shot to telephone Woody and the others. Just wait until they heard *this* idea!

VII

Rancho Hawkins

Harvey drew a chair up to the table in the huge kitchen of Moseley Mansion and flopped down on it.

"May I serve you something to eat or drink, sir?" Hawkins asked.

"Just a glass of water, please," replied Harvey.

"Water, sir?"

"Sure, I like water," said Harvey. He had decided that as long as the Moseley Mansion refrigerator remained practically empty, he would not accept another glass of milk or lemonade, or even another slice of bread and margarine.

"Now, sir," said Hawkins, "you mustn't feel that—"

"Oh, I don't feel anything," said Harvey. "I just really like water a whole lot."

"If you insist, sir," said Hawkins, "but, of course—"

"What I came over to tell you, Hawkins," Harvey said quickly, "is that I won a raffle!"

"You have won a raffle, sir? Oh, I do hope the prize is an—an absolutely splendid one!" Hawkins removed a large green bottle from the refrigerator and began to pour Harvey's water.

"Well, I guess it's splendid, Hawkins," said Harvey. "It's—it's a bunch of chickens."

The water pouring from the green bottle veered to one side the barest fraction of an inch, although not a drop was spilled. "A—a bunch of chickens, sir?"

"Twelve," said Harvey.

Hawkins served Harvey the glass of water and then suddenly his face broke into a thin smile. "Oh, sir! Do you know that for a moment I had the most absurd feeling that you were speaking of *live* chickens!"

"I was," said Harvey. "I mean, I am. I won twelve live chickens from Uncle Doody's cousin's church raffle, Hawkins."

"Live chickens? Oh dear, sir!"

"Don't you like chickens, Hawkins?"

"I find nothing at all wrong with any kind of fowl, sir! On the contrary, they are the most useful of birds," replied Hawkins. "But if I remember correctly, sir, you have long desired to own a furred or feathered pet, but could not because of your younger sister's affliction. I presume you will not be able to keep these chickens unless— unless . . . "

"Unless what, Hawkins?"

"Unless your mother might care to use them for culinary purposes, sir."

"You mean cook them?" gasped Harvey.

"Something along those lines, sir," replied Hawkins. "But please forgive me for mentioning it. I can see that this would be most distressing to you."

"Boy, it sure would, Hawkins! It would—uh— distress me a whole lot. So I guess I'll have to give them back," Harvey said glumly. "Boy, Hawkins, I sure would love to keep one—just *one!*"

"I presume your parents won't allow that, sir?"

"Not one!" cried Harvey. "They say our backyard's not big enough to put enough space between the chickens and Betsy. They said we could keep them if only we had a large yard." Harvey looked up sideways at Hawkins and then returned to gazing dismally into his glass of water. "A very, very, *very* large yard, Hawkins."

"I see, sir."

There was a long silence. Harvey looked up sideways again at Hawkins' face, which remained stiff and expressionless as a dish of dried glue. Harvey took a drink of water.

At last Hawkins spoke. "I believe I know of the existence of a really large yard, sir."

"You do?"

"I refer, sir, to the grounds surrounding Moseley Mansion."

"Wow!" said Harvey. "I never thought of that, Hawkins. You mean keep the chickens here?"

"I mean precisely that, sir."

"Boy, Hawkins, are you sure it won't be too much trouble? I know you know about a lot of stuff, but you've never said anything about keeping chickens."

"I shall make it a point to study their care and habits, sir."

"That's neat, Hawkins! I'll come and help take care of them most of the time, and I'll bet a lot of my friends will help, too. Wow, is it okay if I go and tell them right now?"

Hawkins smiled. "If you wish, sir."

"Gee, thanks for the water, Hawkins!" Harvey drained his glass and raced to the door. He threw it open and then paused.

"Hawkins?"

"Sir?"

"I just happened to think. Suppose some of my chickens lay eggs. I'd want you to have them," said Harvey.

"Oh no, sir, I couldn't possibly take your eggs. I would expect you to take them home."

"Well," said Harvey, "I'll bet when Mom and Dad find out you're going to keep my chickens for me, they won't *let* me bring home any eggs. I'll just bet that if you don't keep the eggs, they won't let you keep my chickens for me. I'll just bet that, Hawkins!"

"Well, put that way, sir. If you absolutely insist."

"I sure do," said Harvey.

"Fresh eggs! Oh, how perfectly splendid!" said Hawkins, drifting. "Fresh eggs, warm from the nest . . . "

Harvey closed the back door of Moseley Mansion softly and hurtled down the driveway toward the tall iron gates. But he had no sooner reached the other side of the gates, out of sight of the mansion, than he was practically knocked over by Woody, Irving, Pinky, David, and Eddy.

"Did he say yes?"

"Is he going to do it?"

Grinning, Harvey nodded.

They all began slapping him on the back.

"That's neat!"

"Oh boy!"

"Wow, Harvey!"

"What did he say about the eggs?" Woody asked.

"Well, he finally said okay, he'd keep the eggs," replied Harvey. "I don't think he guessed anything."

"That's terrific," said Irving.

"You know something?" said Harvey. "I'll bet he didn't guess, because I didn't care so much about the chickens myself as having him keep the eggs."

"Yeah! Maybe you're right, Harvey," said David.

"And something else. If Hawkins gets really hungry—I mean, *really* hungry—then I'll even tell him to—to . . . "

"We know what you mean, Harvey," said Eddy.

"Well, except for Lulu Belle," said Harvey.

"We don't blame you for that," said Irving.

"Gee!" said Harvey. "Just think—Hawkins is going to have his very own chicken ranch!"

"Yeah!" said Woody. "Rancho Hawkins!"

"Maybe some day we can even get him a cow," said Harvey.

"Yeah!" they all said.

VIII

Oh No, Not Again!

"Do you really think it looks okay?" Harvey asked anxiously. "It sure doesn't look like the pictures in the book."

"Nothing ever looks like the pictures in a book," said Woody. "Anyway, remember that contest we entered where it said 'originality counts'? Well, this is pretty original, Harvey."

"Do you really think so?"

"Yeah," said Woody.

The boys were examining what seemed to be a collection of old wooden fruit and vegetable boxes piled up against the Moseley Mansion garage, formerly a coach house.

"It's the neatest looking chicken coop *I've* ever seen," said David.

"Have you seen a whole lot?" asked Harvey.

"Not exactly," David said. "But I did see *one* when I was a little kid, and it was all straight and even and *boring*. This one is really interesting, Harvey. I'll bet the chickens will like it a whole lot."

"I hope so," said Harvey. "But I mostly hope that Hawkins does. Gee, do you think that corner over there needs another nail?"

"Boy, Harvey, if we're not careful, we're going to have more nails than coop," said Woody. "We've already used up the one billion zillion nails you had in your free-thing collection."

"Don't worry, Harvey," Pinky said. "Chickens don't usually run around trying to knock their coops down. Anyway, these are going to be too busy laying eggs for You Know Who." He gave a knowing look in the direction of Moseley Mansion.

"Yeah!" said Harvey. It really made him feel happy every time he thought of those mountains of eggs being laid just for Hawkins. "Golly, Pinky, it was really neat of Uncle Doody and Aunt Bird to give us all those boxes and all that extra wood they had stored in the basement for fence posts. Then they even went and got all that chicken wire for us from Cousin Theodore. Boy oh boy!"

"Well," said Pinky, "after you reported what Mr. Heister is doing to Hawkins, I guess Uncle Doody and Aunt Bird would give practically their whole house to help out!"

"Anyhow," Harvey said, sighing happily, "we ended up getting everything free!"

"Yeah!" said Woody. "Even the worms from Eddy's worm farm, to feed the chickens."

"I wonder what's keeping Eddy and Irving?" David asked. "It sure is taking them a long time to get those worms."

"It sure is," agreed Pinky. "I wish they'd get here so they could help us get the wire up around the chicken yard."

"Hey! Here they come now!" yelled Harvey.

Eddy and Irving had just appeared around the end of the garage lugging Mason jars filled with dirt and worms.

"What kept you so long?" Woody yelled.

"Look, Woody," said Irving. "These worms weren't just lying around Eddy's bedroom, reading comics and watching TV. We had to dig for them."

"Yeah," said Eddy. "And it's a good thing it just rained yesterday so the yard was all muddy and squishy, and the worms were wriggling around. Worms like muddy, squishy stuff."

"Then they'll sure like it here today," said Harvey. "At least until we bring out the chickens. It's muddy and squishy here, too."

"Shall we let them out now, Harvey?" Eddy asked.

"We'd better not," Harvey replied. "We might stomp all over them while we're putting up the chicken wire fence. Anyway, when we've got the fence done and the sign put up, Hawkins can come see all the stuff we've done. We can bring out the worms and the chickens then. It'll be sort of a—a grand opening."

"Yeah!" all the boys agreed.

"But we'd better hurry," said Harvey. "Those poor old chickens have been in those crates in the garage long enough."

Eddy and Irving set the worm jars down carefully, and they all got to work unrolling the chicken wire and hammering it to the posts. The wire was harder to put up than they had thought it would be, and the fence ended up somewhat rickety, with an even more rickety gate. But when they had attached the sign that said *Rancho Hawkins,* everyone decided that, for their first chicken fence, it wasn't too bad.

"Boy, wait until Hawkins sees this!" exclaimed Woody.

"He doesn't have to wait anymore," Harvey said. "Come on, everyone, let's go get him!"

In no time, the boys were back from a trip to Moseley Mansion, bringing Hawkins with them. Anxiously, they all looked at him as he viewed their handiwork.

"Oh, sirs, how—how perfectly splendid!"

"Do you really think so, Hawkins?" asked Harvey anxiously.

"I do indeed, sir! It is unquestionably a most—er—unique home for chickens. Highly—ah—original, if I do say so."

Unique and original? Wow! The boys all turned to one another and grinned.

"Did—did you see the sign, Hawkins?" Woody asked.

"I most assuredly did, sir! *Rancho Hawkins* —I am quite overwhelmed."

"And we did it all ourselves, Hawkins!" Harvey said proudly. "You know, Mom and Dad said that if I let you do one thing to help with my chicken project, back would go the chickens to Uncle Doody's Cousin Theodore. But we've even arranged about feeding them, so you won't have to do that either."

"I brought a bunch of worms from my worm farm," said Eddy, pointing happily to the row of Mason jars on the ground.

"I see, sir," said Hawkins, sounding a little doubtful.

"Is something wrong about feeding chickens worms?" Harvey asked.

"Oh no, sir! It is my understanding that chickens are most particularly delighted with a meal of fresh worms. Twelve is rather a large number of chickens, however, sir, and I'm afraid that . . . "

"You mean you don't think there's enough to go around?" said Harvey.

"Precisely, sir. At least, there would not be enough for more than two or three meals. If you would only allow me, however, to—"

"Golly, no, Hawkins!" said Harvey. "You're not allowed to do anything for these chickens except eat the eggs. We—we'll think of something."

"Are you quite certain, sir?"

"I—I'm certain," said Harvey uncertainly. He had no idea where they would get more food for the chickens, and it was going to be a problem. But for the moment, there were other important things that had to be done.

"Come on, everyone, let's dump the worms into the mud so we can let the chickens out for the grand opening!"

"And while you are preparing the worms and fetching the chickens, sir," said Hawkins, "I shall repair to the kitchen to fetch lemonade."

"But Hawkins," wailed Harvey, "you're not supposed to be giving us stuff to eat or drink. You have to save everything for yourself."

"Yeah, that's right!" agreed the boys.

"Oh, sirs!" said Hawkins, overcome. "How very kind of you! But after all, these chickens represent the very first of either furred or feathered pets that Mr. Harvey Small has ever owned. I cannot allow such an important occasion to pass without some refreshments to help us all celebrate."

"But, Hawkins—," complained Harvey.

"Tut, tut, sir, it is only a little lemonade. Let us hear no more about it. I shall return with it in a moment." And before Harvey could say another word, Hawkins was gone. Anyway, lemonade really did sound like a very neat idea.

"Okay," Harvey shouted, "now we can go ahead with the worms!"

The boys all raced for the jars and began emptying them inside the chicken yard. They waited a few moments for the worms to wiggle their way down into the soft, gooey mud and then started for the garage where the chickens were being kept in their crates. The crates were heavy and ungainly, and even with three boys to a crate, they had to be set down several times before they reached the chicken yard. The boys finally made it, however, and were getting ready to unlatch the

openings to the crates, when suddenly Woody
began to holler.

"Wait, don't open them yet! Don't open them!"

"Why not?" the other boys asked.

"Lollypop's not in my pocket!" moaned Woody.
"He must have fallen out when I was dumping out
a worm jar. A chicken won't know the difference
between a garter snake and a worm. If we don't
find him, it's good-bye Lollypop!"

"Oh gee, Woody!" said Harvey. "What did you
have to go and bring him for?"

"You know I take him just about everywhere.
Come on, everyone, help me find him!" Ignoring
the mud, Woody was down on his hands and
knees, frantically scrabbling around for his pet.
"Careful where you step! Careful where you step!"
he yelled.

The boys were all so intent on looking for
Lollypop that they never even saw the figure that
crept up outside the chicken yard, then dashed in
and unlatched the crate. Several chickens flew out
in a burst of squawks and feathers.

"Who did that?" screamed Woody. "Get 'em!
Get 'em! He-e-elp!"

The whole chicken yard suddenly erupted in a
mass of muddy boys chasing scared, excited
chickens, which scattered to all corners. Woody,
still on his hands and knees, managed to catch one

chicken by the feet, but he saw another one heading toward him. It was at that exact moment that he spotted Lollypop right under his nose.

"Get that chicken, Harvey!" he groaned. "I can't!"

Harvey lunged for the chicken and was just able to snatch it by one foot. At the same time, to keep himself from crashing to the ground, he reached for the post that held the *Rancho Hawkins* sign. All he managed to grab was the sign, which tore off in his hands. So Harvey's feet skidded right out from under him, and he landed on his bottom, sliding across the mud toward Woody. And just then, there was a bright flash of light in the chicken yard! Harvey looked up to see a familiar head of red curls disappearing around the end of the garage. It was then that Hawkins arrived, carrying a large thermos of lemonade and a tray of glasses. He set them down on the ground and ran into the chicken yard where Harvey and Woody lay sprawled, while the other four boys were still chasing the remaining chickens.

"What is it, sir? Whatever has happened?" Hawkins asked.

"It's that Charlotte Grassman, Hawkins!" groaned Harvey. "It looks like she's done it again."

"Oh dear, sir!" said Hawkins.

IX

Chicken Feed

"Well, here we go again, folks—or should we say yolks?" Mr. Small read from the morning *Gazette*. "The two boys who are now old-timers in this column, are fast becoming eggsperts at finding themselves in eggstraordinary situations."

"Oh gee, Dad," groaned Harvey, "do you have to read it out loud?"

"Go on, Daddy, read it! read it!" chirped Betsy happily. She was hanging over her father's shoulder studying the picture in "Chuckle for the Day."

Harvey had already practically studied the picture right off the paper and had read the story at least ten times. He knew it by heart. He also knew that he was going to have to listen to it read at least ten more times by Charlotte Grassman at school. That creepy, sneaky Charlotte and her dumb camera! Harvey jabbed his spoon gloomily into the sea of milk around his morning oatmeal.

Mr. Small read on. "Harvey Small and Woody Woodruff, in their efforts to save Woody's pet garter snake, Lollypop, from a crate of escaping chickens, somehow managed to end up on their rear ends— again! Ouch! This fowl scene was snapped at, of all places, the gardens of Moseley Mansion. It seems that Harvey has established a residence there for his pet chickens, won in a raffle, and named it Rancho Hawkins as we can see from the sign Harvey is waving in the air. The illustrious Hawkins, as some of our readers may know, is the English gentleman's gentleman now in charge of Moseley Mansion. Our thanks again to young Charlotte Grassman, who has provided us with another chuckle for our day. Good going, Charlotte!"

"Good going, Charlotte!" groaned Harvey. "Oh brother!" It was bad enough to be on the receiving end of another "Chuckle for the Day," but to hear that Charlotte Grassman was being handed another medal of honor was more than he could bear.

"Well, if you don't want to have your picture

taken, Harvey, perhaps you should try keeping away from her." Mrs. Small laid a buttered muffin on Harvey's plate.

"How can you keep away from someone like Charlotte, who sticks to you like glue? She sneaked right through those Moseley Mansion gates. Boy, I *told* Eddy and Irving to close them!" Harvey crunched gloomily into his muffin.

"If I had my arms full of jars filled with mud and worms, I don't believe I'd be worrying about closing gates, either," said Mr. Small.

"Anyway, I don't see what's so terrible about getting your picture in the paper." Mrs. Small peered over Mr. Small's shoulder at Harvey's picture on her way to handing him another muffin. "It really is a good likeness, Harvey."

"I'd like to be in 'Chuckle for the Day,' " sang Betsy cheerfully.

"I'm certain a great many of Harvey's friends would, too," said Mrs. Small.

"Not if they had to go around listening to a lot of dumb jokes about their rear ends!" complained Harvey.

"Well, perhaps some day you'll have your picture in the paper doing something really important," said Mr. Small.

"You mean like showing off my collection of famous free things?" said Harvey.

"Er—something like that," said Mr. Small.

"Speaking of worms," said Mrs. Small, changing the subject suddenly, "have you come up with any ideas on how to feed all those chickens, Harvey?"

"I have a few ideas, but I haven't got time to talk about them now," replied Harvey, pushing his chair quickly away from the table. "I have to get ready for school."

Actually, Harvey was as ready for school as he was ever going to be, but he didn't want to reveal to his mother and father that the only idea he had about feeding the chickens was that he didn't really have any ideas. In his room, he flopped at his desk and began to fiddle with the newest addition to his free-thing collection. It was an old flexible watch band, with no flex left in it, that he had found in the empty lot near his home. Fiddling around with one of his free things always helped him to think.

Hawkins had said that the worms from Eddy's worm farm wouldn't take care of Harvey's pet chickens for more than two or three days. So where could he get enough money to buy feed for those chickens? Maybe he should just keep Lulu Belle and send the rest back to Cousin Theodore, Harvey thought. But how many eggs could one chicken provide? And he sure did want those fresh eggs for Hawkins!

Harvey laid down the inflexible watch band and picked up one of the brochures from the small pile on his desk. He really hadn't looked at them since the day Mr. Bunce had given them to Woody and him. What was it Mr. Bunce had said to them about that place up North that kept sending him brochures by the gross? Hadn't they sent him something else, too, like a—like a—?

"Wow!" yelped Harvey. He took a quick look at his desk clock, then leaped up, grabbed his books, and tore down the steps to the front door. If he raced all the way, he had time to make one quick detour before he headed for school.

Harvey stood outside the back door to Moseley Mansion, and pressed the button—for the fifth time. So far, Hawkins had not answered the bright, brisk buzz of the kitchen doorbell. The back door behind the screen door was wide open, so that meant Hawkins must be somewhere around the mansion. It had never taken him more than two rings of the bell to appear before. Could something have happened to him? Harvey opened the screen door and stuck his head in.

"Hawkins? Hawkins?"

There was no answer, so Harvey took a deep breath and stepped in. It really gave him a weird feeling, coming into Moseley Mansion without being let in by that tall, thin figure in the long-tailed black jacket and striped trousers. Where was Hawkins anyway? Harvey crossed the kitchen and went through the pantry, which was larger than his own kitchen at home, and stuck his head through the door to the dining room. It was dim and silent, with the curtains drawn.

"Hawkins? Hawkins!" Harvey called out, but not too loudly, because even the sound of his own voice sounded a little scary in the big, echoing house. The dark mahogany table stared back at him, huge and forbidding. Harvey stepped quickly back into the pantry and ran to the kitchen. He was too scared to go prowling around Moseley Mansion all by himself, and besides, if he spent too much more time there, he'd be late for school. He headed for the back door, but just as he was passing the huge refrigerator, he paused.

Something he had never, ever done was to help himself to anything in the Moseley Mansion kitchen. But then, he wasn't going to help himself to anything now. He just wanted to take a peek inside to see that Hawkins was getting enough to eat. Quickly, he pulled open the refrigerator door. And gasped. The refrigerator was so filled with emptiness you could have built a huge snowman in there and still had space to spare. Poor old Hawkins!

What worried Harvey most was that there were

no eggs in sight. What was wrong with those chickens, anyway? He decided he had better make a quick visit to the chicken yard before starting for school. Hurrying from the kitchen, he raced down the path toward Rancho Hawkins. And that's where he finally found his former gentleman's gentleman, standing in front of the chicken yard holding a small blue pottery bowl heaped with eggs!

"Gee, Hawkins!" cried Harvey. "Did our chickens lay all those?"

"They did indeed, sir!" said Hawkins. "And do you note that egg directly on top?"

"I've noted it, Hawkins," said Harvey. "Wow! A brown egg!"

"Precisely so, sir! And laid, I believe, by the chicken you call—er—Lulu Belle." Hawkins' stiff face actually seemed to melt into a look of wonder as he gazed down at the bowl in his hands. "A whole bowl full of eggs, and even a brown egg, warm from the nest! Sir, I cannot be allowed to keep all these. You must take some home with you."

"I can't do that, Hawkins," said Harvey. "Mom and Dad said that if you keep my chickens, you have to keep the eggs, too."

"Oh, sir!"

Harvey gazed into the chicken yard with pride.

His chickens had done this for Hawkins! Suddenly, however, he noticed something very strange going on in the chicken yard.

"Hawkins, what's that white stuff the chickens are eating? It sure doesn't look like Eddy's worms."

"Just a little something left over from my breakfast, sir," replied Hawkins.

"Gee, Hawkins, you're not supposed to be feeding them your food," said Harvey. He thought of that sad, empty refrigerator he had just looked into.

"It's nothing, sir. Just a few bread crumbs."

"Bread crumbs aren't 'nothing'," said Harvey. "But maybe nobody's going to have to worry about what to feed my chickens anymore. That's what I came to tell you, Hawkins. I just remembered that Mr. Bunce at the pet store has a whole sack of chicken feed he doesn't want, and I'll bet he'll give it to us."

"Oh, that would be splendid, sir!"

"Anyway," Harvey said, "he's going to announce the winner of the puppy this afternoon, and Woody and I are going down there. We can get it then."

"But sir, a sack of chicken feed is entirely too heavy for you and Mr. Woodruff to carry all the way back here," Hawkins said. "Mrs. Moseley would, if she were here, be most happy, I am certain, to allow me the privilege of escorting you and Mr. Woodruff in the automobile to fetch the chicken feed."

"That would be neat, Hawkins!" said Harvey.

"I trusted you might think so, sir," said Hawkins. "In which case, I shall pick you and Mr. Woodruff up at school this afternoon, and any other young persons you might care to invite."

"Wow!" said Harvey.

Imagine being driven to town in that huge black car that Hawkins drove Mrs. Moseley around in! Harvey raced off to try to get to school before the second bell. He just couldn't stand it if he had to wait all that time until recess to tell Woody the big news.

X

A Fantastic Free Thing

The big black car arrived in front of Harvey's school promptly at 3:15 in the afternoon. By 3:16, a swarm of buzzing boys and girls already had packed the sidewalk beside it. A car like that could mean only that someone important was arriving at, or leaving, the school. Nobody, however, so much as put out one finger to touch the bright, shiny finish. It would have taken too much courage to do that to a car, when standing beside it was a tall, thin person in striped trousers, long-tailed black jacket, and gray silk tie with a stickpin in it.

"Gee, Harvey," Woody whispered as they burst through the front door of the school, "we should have sold tickets."

"Yeah," said Harvey. He turned and beckoned to Pinky, Eddy, David, and Irving who were trailing behind them.

"Are you sure it's okay for us to come, Harvey?" asked Pinky.

"Sure it is! Hawkins said to invite any young persons I wanted, and that's you," replied Harvey.

The boys shoved into the crowd around the car.

"Hi, Hawkins!" said Harvey. "We're here."

"So I have observed, sir."

"I asked some young persons, just like you said, Hawkins. Here's Irving, Eddy, Pinky, and David. Is that okay?"

"It is indeed—er—okay, sir. Are you gentlemen all prepared to leave?"

"Yeah!" said the gentlemen.

Hawkins threw open the back door. "Then please step in, sirs!"

Woody, Eddy, David, Pinky, and Irving climbed sedately into the car. They knew that all eyes were on them, and they were feeling very important. Once inside, however, they forgot importance in their excitement over finding real, live jump seats! There was a small scuffle as they decided who would get to sit on them. Woody and Pinky won

out, and David, Eddy, and Irving sank into the huge back seat, where they almost disappeared from sight.

Meanwhile, Harvey still hung around outside the car.

"Don't you wish to enter, sir?" Hawkins asked.

"Oh I'd like to enter, all right," said Harvey, "but up front with you, Hawkins. Is—is that okay?"

"It is not normally *done,* sir, but if you wish it, well then . . ." Hawkins smiled and opened the door to the front seat.

"Thanks, Hawkins!" said Harvey.

"Hey, Harvey!" someone called out from the crowd. "Where are you guys going?"

"Bunce's Pet Store, to find out who won the puppy!" yelled Harvey through the window. But he had no sooner said it than he drew in his breath sharply. "Oh no!"

"Is something wrong, sir?" asked Hawkins quickly.

"I just saw Charlotte Grassman, and I'll bet she heard me. She's running someplace with that camera of hers. I'll bet it's to Bunce's Pet Store!"

"You may well be right, sir. But we cannot let Miss Grassman thwart our purpose. We shall proceed to Bunce's Pet Store as planned, but we shall observe the greatest caution. I assure you, sir, that neither your face nor—er—any other portion of yourself will be featured by Miss Grassman in tomorrow's 'Chuckle for the Day.' "

"Boy, I hope not, Hawkins," said Harvey. Then he decided to forget all about the subject, as the big car purred its way into town. No Charlotte Grassman was going to spoil this ride for him, for anything!

The ride wasn't nearly long enough for Harvey. It seemed no time at all before they were all piling out of the car, a short distance down the street from Bunce's Pet Store.

"Hey!" Woody exclaimed. "What have they done to the lampposts?"

"What does it look like, dopey?" said Eddy. "Somebody painted them."

"Don't you remember, Woody," Harvey said, "that Mrs. Pettit told us there was going to be new paint on the city lampposts? I guess that's what all that modernization and beautification stuff means that Mr. Heister was talking to Mayor Paddle about. It means putting orange paint on everything."

"Yeah, I guess you're right, Harvey," said Woody. "But I think it's kind of weird."

"Yeah," everyone agreed. "It's weird."

"What do you think, Hawkins?" Harvey asked.

"It is a little on the—er—bright and cheerful

side, sir. But what concerns me most at this moment are the large signs stating that the paint is fresh. Assuming that the signs are entirely correct, might I suggest, gentlemen, that we proceed down the street with the utmost care."

"You sure can suggest that, Hawkins," said Harvey. "I don't want any of that orange stuff on *me!*"

"Me neither," said all the boys. "Ugh!"

Then Harvey noticed something else of interest. "Uh-oh! Look over there!"

"Are you referring to the green automobile we are approaching, sir?"

"That's what I'm—ah—referring to, Hawkins," said Harvey. "That's Mayor Paddle's car. He loves hot chocolate better than anything, and I'll bet he's in there at Grandma Goody's Chocolate Shoppe having some right now, just because those dopey lampposts got painted."

"Is there something amiss with sipping hot chocolate to celebrate an event, sir?"

"There's nothing—um—amiss with that, Hawkins. It's just that I bet that Mr. P. M. Heister is in there, too, and I sure don't want to see him."

"Well, gentlemen," said Hawkins, "I'm certain that if we simply proceed on our way to Bunce's, we shall have no unfortunate encounters with Mr. Heister."

Hawkins proved to be right, and they arrived at the pet shop without even seeing Mr. Heister *or* Mayor Paddle. Harvey breathed a sigh of relief.

"Well, you boys are certainly early," Mr. Bunce said as they entered the pet shop. "Didn't skip school, did you?"

The boys all grinned and shook their heads.

"Hawkins drove us here, Mr. Bunce," Harvey said.

"I noticed you had someone with you." Mr. Bunce quickly thrust his hand over the counter. "I suspect you're the famous English gentleman's gentleman I've heard so much about. I'm happy to make your acquaintance, Hawkins!"

"And *I* am most pleased to meet *you*, sir!" said Hawkins. The two gentlemen shook hands warmly.

"We're here because of—because of . . . ," Harvey hesitated. Being given free things, or finding them, was one thing, but *asking* for them was something else. He found it wasn't as easy as he had thought.

"You're here because of the chickens, aren't you?" asked Mr. Bunce matter-of-factly.

Harvey's eyes widened. "How—how did you know?"

"Well, anyone who had seen 'Chuckle for the Day' this morning, and who happened to have a big sack of chicken feed in his back room, could easily guess that, Harvey," said Mr. Bunce. "And please put your wallet away, Hawkins. If Harvey's chickens don't eat the chicken feed, the mice will, and I'm happy to give it away."

"Gee, thanks, Mr. Bunce!" said Harvey.

"Yeah, thanks!" echoed the boys.

"It is very kind of you indeed, sir," said Hawkins.

"Well, it's very kind of *you* to be storing Harvey's chickens for him," said Mr. Bunce. "But I see that the boys and girls are starting to arrive. If you don't mind, I'll announce the winner of the puppy before I go out back for the chicken feed. I'm sure you boys are here to find out about that puppy, too."

The pet shop had been rapidly filling up with girls and boys who had entered the contest. A chorus of oohs and ahs rose as Mr. Bunce lifted the wriggling puppy with soft tan fur and huge floppy ears from its pen in the window and set it on the counter. Then with great deliberation, he pulled the large tablet of yellow paper from the drawer behind the counter and pretended to study it.

"Gee, come on, Mr. Bunce!" someone finally complained. "Tell us who won!"

"Yeah! Tell us! Tell us!" Everyone was dying with the suspense. Everyone wanted that puppy.

"We-e-ell," drawled Mr. Bunce, "it looks as if

the winner is—is Donald Prinkey! Donald guessed five hundred eighty marbles, and the exact number was five hundred seventy-five. Is Donald Prinkey here?"

Donald raised his hand, and just then a light flashed through the store.

"Charlotte Grassman!" exclaimed Harvey. "I knew she'd be here!"

"Well, at least she didn't take a picture of us doing something stupid, Harvey," said Woody.

"Quite right, sir," said Hawkins under his breath. "And if all goes well, you have nothing to fear."

Moans and groans rose in the pet store as Donald Prinkey shoved his way to the counter to retrieve his prize.

"Now you all knew only one person could win the puppy," said Mr. Bunce. "But I'm also giving a second prize. The person who guessed the next closest number of marbles is going to get the marbles. That person, who guessed five hundred fifty, is none other than the Free Thing King, Harvey Small!"

Harvey got lots of applause when he went up for his prize, because nobody minded not winning five hundred seventy-five marbles nearly so much as they minded not winning a cute, wriggling puppy. But just as Harvey took the paper sack of marbles from Mr. Bunce, another light flashed in the store. Harvey just grinned. He didn't mind Charlotte taking his picture when he was receiving a fantastic free thing for his collection. Let her take all the pictures she wanted!

XI

A Fowl Warning

The excitement finally died down, and most of the boys and girls drifted outside, where Donald Prinkey was offering free pats on the puppy's silky head. Then Mr. Bunce called for three volunteers, so Harvey, Pinky, and Woody all disappeared with him into a back room of the pet store. They soon returned, lugging a huge blue and yellow sack of chicken feed, one person to a corner.

"Gee, this is heavy!" groaned Woody. "I'll bet it weighs a zillion trillion pounds."

"Close to that," said Mr. Bunce. "Now, just how is this going to get to Moseley Mansion?"

"In Mrs. Moseley's automobile, which is parked just a few doors down, sir," replied Hawkins. "If you will allow me?" He took hold of Mr. Bunce's corner of the sack, thus relieving him of further duty. "This is indeed a splendid contribution to the cause of fowldom."

"Well, it's high time Harvey had himself some pets," said Mr. Bunce, "even if it is chickens. Let me know if there's anything else I can do for the birds."

Waving to Mr. Bunce, the chicken-feed parade started out. But before they got to the door, Irving shouted, "Hey, Harvey, you left your sack of marbles on the counter. Do you want me to carry it for you?"

Did Harvey? He thought a moment. Someone else could easily take his corner of the chicken-feed sack, and he really did want to carry the marbles. Five hundred seventy-five free things all in one sack—wow!

"Gee, thanks, Irving! But if you'll take my place, I'll get the marbles," said Harvey.

He and Irving changed places. Then, clutching his sack of marbles, Harvey, together with Eddy and David, made a path through the crowd of boys and girls outside the pet store so that Hawkins, Woody, Irving, and Pinky could get through with the chicken feed.

No one was having any trouble carrying the big sack except Woody, who kept groaning and puffing as if he were doing the whole thing all by himself. Then all at once, he hollered, "It's slipping! I have to set it down, everybody! Help!"

Unfortunately, Harvey reacted faster than anyone else. He grabbed Woody's corner of the sack, but in doing so, lost his hold of the sack of marbles. It crashed to the sidewalk and split open. Five hundred seventy-five marbles went rolling in all directions.

At that exact moment, out stepped Mayor Paddle from Grandma Goody's Chocolate Shoppe, followed by Mr. P. M. Heister. Down went one of Mayor Paddle's feet on the marbles. He tried to steady himself with his other foot, but that landed on more marbles. Rolling across the sidewalk as if he were on a skateboard, Mayor Paddle grabbed at the first solid object in his path.

Unluckily, that happened to be a lamppost, freshly painted a bright electric orange. Although his hands slipped around it, he managed to hang on. But his feet finally skidded out from under him. Legs straddling the lamppost, his feet still on the sidewalk, he landed in the gutter with a huge thump. Bright orange paint was smeared all the way from his forehead to his round stomach. Grinning foolishly, he peered around the lamppost.

Unfortunately, he was looking right into the lens of Charlotte Grassman's camera. There was a bright flash of light. Charlotte had done it again, but this time to the mayor himself!

Everything had happened so quickly and so suddenly, that the whole assembled audience stood frozen, watching the mayor roll across the sidewalk and slide down the lamppost. But the camera flash seemed to bring everyone to life.

"Oh, sir!" exclaimed Hawkins, as he and the boys quickly lowered the sack of chicken feed to the sidewalk. "Allow me to be of assistance." He was at Mayor Paddle's side in an instant.

But so was Mr. P. M. Heister. "You have already been of *enough* assistance, Hawkins!" he said angrily. "*I* will take care of this."

He grabbed Mayor Paddle's arm and tugged and tugged, but accomplished little more than getting a lot of orange paint on himself. The portly mayor seemed destined to remain in the gutter, draped around the lamppost forever.

"Well, you might as well help me, Hawkins," Mr. Heister said ungraciously.

With Hawkins' help, the puffing Mayor Paddle was soon back on his feet.

"This is all your doing, Hawkins," said Mr. Heister through tight lips.

"No it's not!" cried Harvey. "I was the one

carrying the sack of marbles, and I dropped them!"

Mr. Heister turned and stared at Harvey. "Oh it's *you*, the one who's always getting into mischief. Well, run along, little boy, this is none of your affair. Shoo! Shoo!" He waved Harvey off as if Harvey were one of his chickens.

"I accept full responsibility, sir," said Hawkins.

"It's all right, P. M.," whispered Mayor Paddle. He was looking very embarrassed and uncomfortable. "It's only a little paint, and I wasn't hurt at all."

"It certainly is not all right, Your Honor," said Mr. Heister. "Your image! Your image!"

"Pooh on my image!" said Mayor Paddle under his breath. But he seemed too afraid to say it aloud to Mr. Heister.

Mr. Heister turned back to Hawkins. "Furthermore, I thought I warned you that your job at Moseley Mansion did not include any outside activities with these children. What, pray tell, are you doing with them?"

Not a muscle moved on Hawkins' face. "*This* is my afternoon off, sir."

"Well—well—," stammered Mr. Heister. "Well, since you are here, this saves me coming to see you later, as I had planned." He whipped from his pocket a copy of "Chuckle for the Day" clipped from the newspaper, and thrust it under Hawkins' nose. "I want to know the meaning of this—this Rancho Hawkins. Are you raising chickens now at Moseley Mansion?"

"The chickens are a young boy's pets, sir," replied Hawkins.

"Well, whatever they are, you weren't employed to look after chickens, and I'm sure they're taking up a great deal of your time."

"Not at all, sir. The lad and his friends have built the coop and chicken yard entirely on their own, and they take entire charge of the chickens, including providing their food, as you can see here."

"Humph!" snorted Mr. Heister. "I can see all right. A big sack of chicken feed and a lot of little boys being driven around royally in Mrs. Moseley's car. Anyway, none of this is important, because there's a law against keeping chickens in—"

Mr. Heister's remarks were cut short by Mayor Paddle, looking more miserable and uncomfortable by the moment, who began to tug at his sleeve.

"There isn't any law, P. M.," whispered the mayor.

Mr. Heister's eyebrows flew up on his forehead. "None at all?"

"N-n-none that I know of," stammered the poor mayor.

"Well, we'll have to see about that," said Mr.

Heister coldly. "Now, where is that little girl who took the picture? Oh, there you are! Little girl, let me have that camera, please."

Charlotte stepped away from him, shaking her head and clutching her camera.

"Little girl, I want that camera!" said Mr. Heister, his face turning deep red with anger.

Charlotte began to look frightened, but she clearly had no thought of giving in. "No! No, you can't have it!" she cried. Then she turned suddenly and began to run.

"Stop her! Stop her!" screeched Mr. Heister, but nobody bothered to do it.

"If that picture gets into 'Chuckle for the Day' . . . " Mr. Heister gritted his teeth. "Hawkins, I'm warning you! Well, we shall leave before any further disasters take place. Come along, Your Honor."

"Gee Hawkins," said Harvey when it was all over, "maybe Charlotte will give the *Gazette* the picture of me and my marbles, instead of the one of Mayor Paddle."

"I doubt that that will happen, sir—most unfortunately!"

"Boy!" breathed Harvey. "Mr. Heister is really out to get you, Hawkins."

"I am afraid so, sir. I am afraid so," said Hawkins.

XII

A Law Is a Law

"Gee, Mom and Dad, why can't I ask Hawkins to come with Woody and me to the movies? Why can't I?" Harvey pleaded at the dinner table.

"Because we think you've pestered Hawkins enough," replied Mrs. Small. "Not to mention all the trouble he's been in because of you boys. Why can't you and Woody go to the Saturday matinee? Then you wouldn't need anyone to go with you."

"Tonight is the last time we can use those free passes Uncle Doody just gave us, that's why," replied Harvey. "Please can I ask Hawkins?"

"I can't imagine that Hawkins would really want to see this movie, Harvey," said Mr. Small.

"He told me that it—it would be *splendid* to go with Woody and me," Harvey said.

"You mean to *Fango and the Space Patrol?*" Mr. Small looked faint. "Well, that just goes to prove what I've been thinking. Hawkins probably would go to any length to please you, Harvey."

Betsy giggled, and Harvey threatened her with a look.

"Are you quite sure about this, Harvey?" asked Mrs. Small.

"Sure, I'm sure. Besides, Hawkins is sitting there all by himself in that big old house. I'll bet he'd like to go to *any* old movie."

"Well, this is certainly any old movie," said Mr. Small.

"Who would buy Hawkins' ticket?" asked Mrs. Small. "You certainly wouldn't expect *him* to—"

"Heck, no!" exclaimed Harvey. "Pinky got a free pass, too, but he's already seen *Fango and the Space Patrol,* so he gave us his pass for Hawkins. But Woody and I are going to *buy* Hawkins an ice-cream cone at Grandma Goody's!"

Mr. Small looked at Mrs. Small. "They certainly have this mission all planned out."

"Then is it okay?" asked Harvey excitedly.

Mrs. Small sighed. "We-e-ell . . ."

"Gee, thanks!" Harvey was up the stairs before his mother could even make up her mind what she was going to say next.

"Boy, this cherry chip is a neat flavor!" Harvey said. He and Woody and Hawkins had just left Grandma Goody's and were on their way to the Regal Theater.

"Yeah!" agreed Woody.

"It's too bad you just got boring old chocolate, Hawkins," said Harvey.

"If you'll excuse me for saying so, sir," replied Hawkins, "there is no such thing as—er—boring old chocolate. Especially when it is presented in a form which has never been tried before."

Harvey and Woody both turned to Hawkins with wide eyes. "You mean you've never had an ice-cream cone before, Hawkins?"

"Precisely, sir."

"Wow, Woody!" exclaimed Harvey. "We just bought Hawkins his very first ice-cream cone!"

"Yeah, wow!" agreed Woody.

They proceeded down the street, licking their cones.

"Hey, look!" Harvey pointed across the street at a solitary light shining in an upstairs corner of an otherwise darkened building. "Somebody sure is working late over there."

"What building is that, sir?" asked Hawkins.

"That's the town hall, Hawkins," Harvey replied. "The room with the light in it is where all the important papers and old law books are stored. I remember from fourth grade, when we went to the town hall on a field day. It's right next to Mayor Paddle's office."

"Hmmm, I see, sir," said Hawkins thoughtfully.

"It sounds like you see something weird about that," said Harvey. "Do you, Hawkins?"

"Oh no, no!" Hawkins said quickly. "Nothing—ah—weird at all, sir. Well, here we are at the cinema, gentleman! And right on time, I trust." He seemed to have forgotten all about the lighted window.

"Boy, I trust so, too, Hawkins," said Harvey. "I sure would hate to miss any of this neat movie."

"Yeah!" breathed Woody rapturously. *"Fango and the Space Patrol—*wow!"

In a daze, the boys passed under the bright, flashing neon sign of the Regal Theater and were soon lost in another world, composed of plush seats, popcorn, and a big silver screen. Two and a half hours later, they returned to earth.

"Wow!" said Harvey.

"Yeah, wow!" agreed Woody.

"I wish it could have gone on forever," said Harvey.

"Yeah, forever," agreed Woody.

"Gee, Hawkins," Harvey said, "we're sure glad you could come with us tonight. I would have died if I couldn't have seen this movie."

"That would have been most unfortunate, sir."

"Aren't you glad you came?" Harvey asked.

"Oh, I am indeed, sir!" replied Hawkins. "It was a—a truly—er—*splendid* film!"

"I thought you'd think so," said Harvey.

Then, as they left the theater, Harvey noticed something. "Hey, that light in the town hall is out! I guess whoever it was, finished his business and left."

"If I might make a correction, sir, I believe the person is just leaving now."

"Uh-oh!" exclaimed Harvey under his breath. "It's Mr. P. M. Heister!"

"As I had feared, sir!"

"Hadn't we better hide?" Harvey asked anxiously. "I sure don't want him to see you with Woody and me, Hawkins. Mom says you've been in enough trouble because of us."

"It is kind of your mother to be concerned, sir, but tonight is my evening off, and if I choose to spend it seeing—ah—*Fango and the Space Patrol* with my friends, that is my privilege. In any event, Mr. Heister seems not to be noticing what is going

on on this side of the street, so I believe we have
nothing to fear."

They watched in silence as Mr. Heister paused
for a moment under one of his bright orange
lampposts. Wearing a strange smile, he pulled out
his pocket watch and studied it. He appeared to be
waiting for someone. Mayor Paddle? Harvey wondered. But it was not the familiar stout figure of
the mayor that finally materialized from the sha-
dows. It was a strange man Harvey had never seen
before. The stranger held a short, animated conference with Mr. Heister, and then the two hurried
off together.

"Gee, what was that all about?" asked Harvey.

"I'm afraid I do not know, sir," replied Hawkins. "But it does not bode well for Mr. Heister to
be burning the midnight oil, so to speak, reviewing
the town's old records."

"Do you know what he was looking for,
Hawkins?"

"I cannot even hazard a guess, sir. But whatever
it was, I very much fear that we are going to hear
about it all too soon. All too soon, indeed!"

"Boy, soon is right, Hawkins!" exclaimed Harvey. Only it was now early the following morning,
and Harvey was in the chicken yard at Moseley
Mansion, tending his chickens. Hawkins, in his

work apron and carrying a basket heaped with rags and polishes, had stopped a moment to say good morning to Harvey, when a familiar bright green car rolled up the driveway and pulled to a stop. Out hopped an eager Mr. Heister, followed by Mayor Paddle, who hoisted himself heavily from the car looking as if he would prefer to be anywhere else in the world but here.

"Well, Hawkins, I had thought you were to have nothing to do with these chickens at—at Rancho Hawkins." Mr. Heister's voice dripped with meanness and sarcasm.

"He—he isn't having anything to do with them!" cried Harvey. "He was on his way to polish Mrs. Moseley's car."

"It doesn't matter what Hawkins was on his way to do, little boy. The chickens have to go, anyway." Mr. Heister whipped a piece of paper from his briefcase and waved it under Hawkins' nose. "Here!" he announced triumphantly. "It's all right here—a copy of the chicken law. I knew I'd finally find one!" Mr. Heister was almost gleeful. "What it says is that chickens can't be raised in any yard within the town limits. Isn't that so, Your Honor?"

"I—I suppose it is," replied Mayor Paddle. His triple chins all quivered with dismay. The mayor looked as if he would give ten years of his life if he did not have to enforce any chicken law. "Of course, it's a very, very *old* law," he added glancing sideways at Mr. Heister.

"A law is a law, Your Honor," snapped Mr. Heister, shriveling Mayor Paddle with a look.

"But sir," said Hawkins, "if I might be allowed an observation, we are not raising chickens here at Moseley Mansion. These are a lad's pets."

"Come, come, Hawkins," said Mr. Heister testily. "Let's not bandy words. Chickens are chickens, and these have got to go. I will expect you to make arrangements to get rid of them at once." Then he lowered his voice to keep Mayor Paddle from hearing. "If you don't approve of this, you are certainly free to leave."

"But, Mr. Heister—," Harvey blurted.

"At *once*, Hawkins!" commanded Mr. Heister. "Now come along, Your Honor, we are late for our appointment to see about painting the school windows."

He turned on his heel and marched off. Mayor Paddle quavered a smile at Hawkins and Harvey and then, looking thoroughly beaten down and unhappy, trailed after Mr. Heister.

"Get rid of the chickens?" moaned Harvey. "H-h-how, Hawkins?"

"Do not be distressed, sir. Getting rid of chickens does not necessarily mean—ah—doing away with them. It could mean finding a home for them outside the town, somewhere in the country, perhaps, sir."

"Gee, Hawkins, that's right!" cried Harvey. "And I've already thought of a place. Uncle Doody's Cousin Theodore's! It's where the chickens came from, and maybe he'll take them back."

"Oh sir, that is indeed a splendid idea!"

"Yeah, I guess it is pretty—uh—splendid," said Harvey, "But—but—"

"But what, sir? Are you concerned about missing your pets?"

Visiting his chickens, however, wasn't what was worrying Harvey. What he was worried about was that Hawkins would not have any more free eggs for that big, empty refrigerator. But Harvey couldn't say so, because he had to remember Hawkins' gentleman's gentleman's pride. He would have to wait and discuss the problem with Woody and his other friends later.

"Yeah, that's what I'm—er—concerned about, Hawkins," said Harvey.

"Oh sir, I am certain that if Mr. Patterson's cousin adopts the chickens, he will allow you to visit them frequently."

"I guess you're right, Hawkins. Anyway, now we know what Mr. Heister was doing at the town hall so late the other night. He was looking up old chicken laws!"

"That does seem to be the case, sir. Mr. Heister seems to be of the opinion that, if he badgers me enough, I might leave Moseley Mansion."

"Boy, I sure hope you don't!" exclaimed Harvey.

"That is not my present intent, sir."

"But why was Mr. Heister meeting that strange man so late at night, Hawkins?" Harvey asked. "I'll bet that didn't have anything to do with chickens."

"I am afraid you may be right, sir. I believe the strange gentleman has to do with something far more dastardly than merely doing away with a few harmless birds. I fear we shall hear more of him soon."

"Wow!" said Harvey.

"Precisely so, sir," replied Hawkins.

XIII

Town Hall, Ta-Ta!

"Gee, Harvey, what are we going to do?" Pinky asked.

Irving sighed. "Poor old Hawkins!"

"With no more eggs!" said David.

Eddy shook his head sadly. "That big, empty refrigerator!"

"Harvey, we have to do *something!*" said Woody.

"Boy oh boy, Woody," said Harvey, "don't you think I know?"

Harvey had called a conference as soon as he returned from Moseley Mansion, and the boys were now all sitting in his room discussing the terrible situation.

"Well, at least we don't have to worry about your chickens, Harvey," Pinky said. "I'm pretty sure Cousin Theodore will take care of them for you."

"Hey!" Irving slapped his forehead excitedly. "I just thought of something. If Cousin Theodore has the chickens, maybe he can bring Hawkins the eggs whenever he comes in to see Uncle Doody."

Woody, David, Eddy, and Pinky all grinned. "Hey, yeah, Irving!"

But Harvey shook his head. "No, Hawkins wouldn't take them. He only takes the eggs now because he knows my mom and dad wouldn't let him keep my chickens at Moseley Mansion if he didn't. He'd never take the eggs if somebody else was keeping the chickens. It's his—"

"Yeah, Harvey, we know," Irving broke in. "His gentleman's gentleman's pride. You're right, he'd never take them."

"Yeah," they all agreed.

"Well, what are we going to do?" Pinky asked again.

Everyone looked at everyone else and shrugged. They all sat with fists under their chins, thinking. Nobody paid much attention to the doorbell ringing below, but a few moments later, Mrs. Small appeared in Harvey's room.

"Harvey, Charlotte Grassman is here to see you."

"Charlotte Grassman!" exploded Harvey. "Well, I don't want to see *her.*"

"You can't be rude, Harvey," replied Mrs. Small. "I think you ought at least to come and see what she wants."

"Gee, Mom—"

"I'll tell her you'll be right down," said Mrs. Small, and promptly disappeared.

Harvey exchanged raised-eyebrow glances with Woody, Pinky, Irving, Eddy, and David. Everyone there knew that Harvey had to go whether he liked it or not. "We-e-ell," he said, "I'll just go down and tell her good-bye."

"You'd better watch out going down the stairs, Harvey," Woody warned him. "I'll bet she's already got her camera aimed right at them."

Harvey wasn't going to take any chances. He went down the stairs very, *very* slowly, dragging his feet. Maybe Charlotte would even give up and go home. But she was waiting by the front door when he arrived. She looked a little scared. And she didn't even have her camera with her.

"I came to tell you I'm sorry I took those pictures!" she blurted.

Harvey's jaw fell. Charlotte Grassman making

apologies was not what he had expected. "That's —that's okay," he stammered.

"No, it isn't," insisted Charlotte. "At least not the second picture. That one wasn't even fair. *I* let the chickens out of the crate, and that was cheating. I told my mother about what happened in town, and she thinks maybe I got Hawkins in trouble with Mr. Heister over that picture. My mother doesn't like Mr. Heister at all."

By the time this breathless speech had been ended all in one rush, Charlotte the Enemy had suddenly become Charlotte the Friend.

"Nobody likes Mr. Heister," said Harvey as calmly as if the person responsible for his being in "Chuckle for the Day" was a million miles away.

"But *is* Hawkins in trouble about the picture?" asked Charlotte.

"Sort of," replied Harvey. "Once Mr. Heister found out about the chickens through the picture, he dug up an old chicken law that says you can't raise chickens in the town limits. He came out with Mayor Paddle to tell Hawkins about it. So I guess the chickens have got to go."

"I'm sorry," said Charlotte. "But the chickens don't belong to Hawkins, do they? Aren't they *your* pets?"

"Yeah," said Harvey, "but—but—"

"But what?" asked Charlotte.

And then Harvey told her the whole story of how the chickens came to be at Moseley Mansion, and how important it was for Hawkins to have the eggs because Mr. Heister was hardly paying him any wages. Harvey even explained about Hawkins' gentleman's gentleman's pride, and what a problem it had all become.

"Oh, poor Hawkins!" exclaimed Charlotte. "What are you going to do about it, Harvey?"

"I don't know. A law is a law, Charlotte. That's what Mr. Heister said, and I guess he's right. Anyway, Mayor Paddle thinks so."

"That Mayor Paddle!" cried Charlotte, tossing her head angrily. "He could do something about changing a dumb old chicken law if he really wanted to. My mother thinks he's turning into an old dodo and he ought to be ashamed of himself. She says he's covering up all the town problems with orange paint just because Mr. Heister tells him to."

"I think he *is* a *little* ashamed of himself," said Harvey, remembering the hang-dog, embarrassed expression on Mayor Paddle's face.

"Then maybe he just thinks nobody is noticing all the stuff that's going on, Harvey. Maybe somebody ought to tell him." Charlotte bobbed her head determinedly.

"But how?" asked Harvey. "We can't just go up to Mayor Paddle and tell him he's a dodo."

"No, but—but . . . " Charlotte bit her lip, thinking. "I think there is a way that we can do it."

"How"

"March on town hall," said Charlotte matter-of-factly.

"M-m-march on town hall?" squeaked Harvey.

Charlotte nodded.

"You mean just *us?*" Harvey's voice squeaked again.

"Not just you and me," replied Charlotte. "We'll get a whole bunch of kids to let Mayor Paddle know we don't like Mr. Heister's old chicken laws. Next thing, Harvey, he'll be digging up some old puppy laws and kitten laws."

"Yeah, that's right," said Harvey. "But when are we going to—march?"

"We ought to do it right away," replied Charlotte. "But we'll have to get all our friends to help."

"Gee!" said Harvey. "Woody, David, Irving, Pinky, and Eddy are up in my room right now. We were talking about how we could help Hawkins."

"That's terrific!" exclaimed Charlotte. Her eyes sparkled. "We can tell them right now."

Harvey hesitated. "The only thing is—is—"

"Is what?" asked Charlotte.

"Well, we can march on town hall all right," replied Harvey. "But we can't let anyone except my friends know we're really marching because of

Hawkins. You know he might find out and—and—"

"I know—Hawkins' gentleman's gentleman's pride," said Charlotte.

Harvey grinned. Good old Charlotte Grassman!

"Sir, do you really think you should be doing this?" Hawkins asked. "It would seem to me that—"

Hawkins opinion was halted in mid-sentence by noisy squawking and the sound of wings flapping as Harvey, Woody, Eddy, and Pinky tried to shove six nervous chickens into a crate.

"It's just a bunch of us kids going to —um—*visit* Mayor Paddle," said Harvey. "Charlotte thinks it would help a lot to have some chickens with us."

"If you'll excuse me for saying so, sir," replied Hawkins, "though I think your friendship with Miss Grassman is simply splendid, I wonder if she is not perhaps a little too—er—enterprising. Perhaps you should reconsider . . . "

Harvey pushed an anxious chicken's head back down into the crate. "Maybe she is what you said, Hawkins, but *I* think we should take some chickens, too. It will make our—uh—visit more newsworthy. That's what Charlotte says."

"They are your chickens, sir, to do with as you will," said Hawkins, "but please do exercise the utmost care when visiting His Honor, the Mayor."

"Oh, we'll do the exercising all right, Hawkins," said Harvey. "You don't have to worry."

Still, Hawkins didn't look too cheerful when the four boys finally left for the city park, lugging the big crate filled with chickens.

About thirty boys and girls were already gathered in a far corner of the town park when Harvey, Woody, Eddy, and Pinky arrived with the crate. Charlotte ran up to them at once.

"You got the chickens!" she said excitedly. "Now I guess we can start."

"You aren't taking your camera with you, are you?" Harvey eyed suspiciously the camera Charlotte had hanging from a strap around her neck.

"Sure!" said Charlotte. "But don't worry, Harvey, I'm not going to take any funny pictures today. I'm just going to take some for the article my mother is going to write for the *Gazette* about our march. She's going to be at town hall today."

"Wow, that's neat!" said Harvey.

"Okay, everyone!" Charlotte shouted. "Harvey is here with his chickens. So off to town hall, ta-ta!"

Harvey, Woody, Eddy, and Pinky led the way with the chicken crate. Beside them marched a determined Charlotte with her camera ready, and behind them followed all the other boys and girls, waving their signs in the air:

PADDLE HATES PETS!
SAVE HARVEY'S CHICKENS!
FOWL IS NOT A DIRTY WORD!
NIX ON CHUCKING CHIX!
PHOOEY ON OLD CHICKEN LAWS!
SAVE OUR PETS!

There were other signs too:

PADDLE PAINTS POSTS WHILE KIDS
  FREEZE!
ORANGE PAINT DOES NOT KEEP OUT
  DRAFTS!
BUY BOOKS, NOT PAINT BRUSHES!
YOU CAN'T READ A LAMPPOST!
FIDDLE-FADDLE, MAYOR PADDLE!

Town hall was only a block from the park, but the marchers picked up a lot of followers and onlookers along the way. When they finally arrived at the red brick building with the tall white pillars, even more people, both grown-ups and children, began to collect. There was quite a crowd in front of town hall.

Two of the people there were dressed in white overalls and caps. They were painters who were putting a second coat of paint on the pair of lampposts in front of the building. They glanced nervously over their shoulders, but soon discovered that although there were a lot of smart remarks from the gathering, nobody was going to bother them. They went on painting.

The four boys set the crate of chickens down at the foot of the wide steps to the town hall door. Then Harvey stood guard over his chickens while Woody, Eddy, and Pinky joined their friends as they began to march up and down in front of the building. The crowd around them offered all kinds of encouragement.

"Go get 'em, kids!"

"Hey, those chickens will cook Mayor Paddle's goose!"

"Don't let 'em get those birds, Harvey!"

Neither Mayor Paddle nor Mr. Heister, however, had so far put in an appearance. But after a short while, the doors of Town Hall opened, and a breathless, pink-cheeked young woman came flying down the steps. She stopped right beside Harvey.

"You—you children have all had a good time, and now—now Mr. Heister would like you to please—please leave," she stammered.

"Tell Mr. Heister to come out himself and order them off!" someone hollered from the crowd.

"He can't do that," someone else replied. "He's too chicken!" This brought a big laugh from the gathering.

"Well . . . well . . . ," said the flustered young woman. She looked as if she were about to cry.

The marching boys and girls weren't quite certain what to do, but they all stopped and looked at Harvey as if *he* ought to be saying something. And it was in that split second while Harvey was thinking, that two boys he didn't even know, darted from the crowd. Before Harvey or anyone else knew what they were up to, they had opened the flap on the crate and dumped out the contents. There was a sudden explosion of squawking chickens and flying feathers everywhere. The orderly march on town hall suddenly broke into a confused mass of people chasing chickens, chickens flying into lampposts and leaving deposits of feathers on the wet paint, paint tins being knocked over, and rivers of orange paint spreading down the street. Chickens and orange paint were everywhere.

Then suddenly, Harvey was both relieved and horrified to see a familiar tall, thin figure materialize in the crowd.

"Hawkins!" he cried. "What are you doing here?"

"I came, sir, to persuade you against coming here, as I feared the worst from the enterprise."

"But I didn't want you to come, Hawkins. You're already in enough trouble because of me," moaned Harvey.

134

"Well, the fact of the matter is, sir, that I am here, so let us get on with the matter of restoring order before it is too late."

But the fact of the matter was that it was already too late. This time it was not the secretary, but Mr. Heister himself who came bursting through the town hall doors in a towering rage, followed by a red-faced, distraught Mayor Paddle.

"You children will all be punished for this," shrieked Mr. Heister. "You will pay to have the lampposts repainted! You will pay for all the paint! You will pay to have the streets cleaned! You will pay for— Aha!" Mr. Heister's shifting eyes had suddenly discovered something. "So it's *you*, Hawkins! You're at the bottom of this! Well, let me tell you something. I don't have to go looking up any laws about disturbing the peace. We *do* have one of those, don't we, Mayor?" He looked down his angry nose at Mayor Paddle.

"Y-y-yes," replied poor Mayor Paddle nervously. "B-b-but we've never had to use it."

"A law does not have to be used to be a law," snapped Mr. Heister. "Hawkins has broken a law, and he must be punished."

"But—but this wasn't Hawkins fault," blurted Harvey. "We kids were the ones who planned it all. Hawkins tried to talk us out of it."

"Well," sneered Mr. Heister, "he didn't talk hard

135

enough, now, did he? Which is as good as saying he was all for it."

"I assume the entire blame, sir," said Hawkins.

"But Hawkins—," cried Harvey.

"Well now," Mr. Heister, paying no attention whatsoever to Harvey, "I'm glad you intend to be reasonable about this, Hawkins. In which case, I'm sure Mayor Paddle will agree with me that you should be given your choice of punishment. Ten days in jail—or ten days to leave town!"

Hawkins never so much as flickered an eyelash. "Very good, sir!"

"Oh no!" groaned Harvey.

XIV

Farewell

The following morning's *Gazette* featured a picture of the children marching in front of town hall. A second picture showed a worried Mayor Paddle, a furious Mr. P. M. Heister, an English butler with a face as stiff as a bottle of dried glue, and a ten-year-old boy who looked as if he were about to burst into tears. Both pictures had been taken by Charlotte Grassman to go with an article written by her mother.

CHILDREN MARCH ON TOWN HALL

MOSELEY MANSION BUTLER GIVEN TEN DAYS IN JAIL OR TEN DAYS TO LEAVE TOWN FOR DISTURBING PEACE

Yesterday afternoon, a group of children marched on town hall in defense of their rights to keep chickens as pets.

Twenty-five boys and girls led by Harvey Small and his friends descended on Town Hall after school yesterday to let Mayor Paddle know they did not appreciate his enforcement of an old law, diligently dug up by his assistant, Mr. P. M. Heister. The law states that chickens cannot be raised in any yard within the town limits. Harvey Small, owner of the chickens in question, had been generously permitted by Hawkins, the English butler employed by Mrs. Margaret Moseley, to keep the chickens at Moseley Mansion. The children claim that Harvey's chickens are pets, and that he is not in the business of raising anything. They fear that someday they will be told they cannot keep any pets at all.

In addition to the chicken law, the children are also protesting Mayor Paddle's campaign to "beautify" and "modernize" the town with orange paint. They say that Mayor Paddle should remember his promise to fix their drafty school windows and buy new books for their school library, and not spend his time (and the town's money!) on orange paint and digging up old chicken laws.

The children's march, unfortunately, ended in chaos when two young mischief-makers opened the crate containing some of Harvey's chickens and let them out into the crowd. Hawkins valiantly claimed the blame for the disaster, over Harvey's protests. Mr. P. M. Heister, in this reporter's opinion, seemed overly quick to accept Hawkins' word, and, on the spot, offered him the choice of ten days in jail or ten days to leave town. Hawkins is a popular figure hereabouts, and his departure would be regrettable. It is hoped that justice will be done.

Mr. Small simply sat and shook his head over the article when he had finished reading it aloud at the breakfast table.

"Gee, Mom and Dad," Harvey groaned, "isn't there anything *we* can do?"

"Harvey, I intend to speak to Mr. Heister, but I'm afraid he will be determined that justice, as *he* sees it, be done."

"How about Mayor Paddle?" asked Harvey. "Couldn't he do something? I think he likes Hawkins."

"I am sure he does," replied Mr. Small. "But poor old Mayor Paddle seems to be thoroughly frightened by Mr. Heister. I don't think we can look for much help from him."

"Maybe something magic will happen to save Hawkins," Betsy piped up.

Harvey was too downcast even to curl up his lip at her. Anyway, he was sort of hoping for something magical or miraculous himself, because that seemed to be the only hope left.

Ten days later, however, nothing magical, miraculous, or anything else had happened to change the situation. Hawkins was leaving, and Harvey, carrying a long, flat package tucked under his arm, was on his way to Moseley Mansion to see him for the last time.

Harvey had been growing a little more accustomed to the grayness and ghostliness of the mansion, and he really did like the old place. Think of all the historic events that had taken place there! But today, because Harvey knew that Hawkins would soon no longer be there, the mansion seemed to loom over him, grayer and ghostlier than ever.

The chickens were gone, too. Harvey hesitated at the place where the driveway turned off toward the garage and the back door, wondering if he should try the front door today. He couldn't bear to pass by the garage where his chickens had once been. There was nothing there now but dust and a few lonely chicken feathers blowing about.

Then, as he stood wondering which direction to take, he noticed something strange at the front of the mansion. There were a lot of wooden folding chairs set up right in front of the porch leading to the front door. On the porch was something that looked like a podium. Was somebody coming to make a farewell speech for Hawkins? Harvey wondered. Why hadn't anybody told *him?* Then suddenly two men appeared from around the opposite side of the mansion. They were holding a deep discussion and didn't notice Harvey. But Harvey noticed *them,* all right. They were Mr. Heister and the man he had met in front of the town hall lamppost on the night Mr. Heister had been busy looking up old chicken laws!

Harvey didn't need to stand around anymore making up his mind which door he should try. He wheeled around and tore down the drive leading to the back door. He was still gasping for breath when Hawkins answered the doorbell.

"Oh sir, how perfectly splendid of you to come!"

"I wouldn't have not come for anything, Hawkins," said Harvey. "You're practically my best friend."

"Oh, sir!" said Hawkins, overcome. "But you've been running, sir. There was no need to hurry. I still have some time before I must leave. Please, won't you enter?"

"I know that," said Harvey, entering. "I was running because—because of someone I just saw in front of Moseley Mansion."

Hawkins suddenly looked grim. "I believe I know the people to whom you refer, sir. They are Mr. Heister and the gentleman we noted him meeting on the evening you and Mr. Woodruff were so kind as to invite me to the screening of *Fango and the Space Patrol*."

Harvey was startled. "You mean you've seen them too?"

"I have indeed, sir. They have been—*snooping* about the property since early this morning."

"Well, they don't have to snoop about the chickens," said Harvey indignantly. "They're gone!"

"I know that, sir. My conclusion is that they must be here on some business having to do with the auction of Moseley Mansion."

"Auction of Moseley Mansion?" exploded Harvey. "You—you mean it's going to be sold?"

"I am afraid so, sir."

"Is that what all those chairs are doing out in front?" Harvey asked.

"I believe so, sir, since the auction is to be held within the hour."

"Within the hour?" Harvey was dumbfounded.

"But—but how come I didn't know about it before?"

"It is my opinion, sir, that very few people knew about it, including myself."

"Anyway, what would Mr. Heister and his friend have to do with selling Moseley Mansion?" asked Harvey.

"You may recollect, sir, that some time ago I spoke to you of my suspicion that skulduggery was afoot?"

Harvey nodded. "I sure do recollect that, Hawkins. You said you thought someone wanted you out of the way too, so they could do a bunch of underhanded stuff, but you were going to stick around until you found out what it was."

"Your recollection is quite correct, sir. My suspicion now is that the sale of Moseley Mansion is exactly that—er—underhanded stuff, and that it was somehow masterminded by Mr. P. M. Heister and Co. and will result in something to their advantage. You will note too, sir, that the sale coincides with my departure, so I am no longer able to—ah—stick around and make any unpleasant discoveries."

"Oh brother!" said Harvey.

"Precisely so, sir."

"But—but what about Mrs. Moseley? Why isn't she here if Moseley Mansion is going to be sold?" Harvey asked.

"Perhaps she is still gravely ill, sir. I must confess, however, that I have the curious feeling Mrs. Moseley does not know about the sale at all."

"Then why don't *you* tell her about it?" Harvey said excitedly.

"I'm afraid it is much too late, sir. Besides, under the circumstances I—I don't feel that—"

"You mean that stuff about having to leave town or go to jail, Hawkins?"

"That is unfortunately what I do mean, sir. I'm afraid that my—my—"

Harvey sighed. "I know, Hawkins. Your gentleman's gentleman's pride wouldn't let you do it. Boy, it's all my fault too. Me and my dopey chickens and the dumb chicken march on town hall."

"Sir!"

Harvey drew back. Never had he heard such a stern tone in Hawkins' voice, and never had he seen Hawkins' face look so stiff and forbidding.

"You must never speak of that again, sir!" said Hawkins.

Harvey's insides shriveled. Hawkins must really be mad at him about those chickens, so mad he couldn't even accept an apology! "I—I w-w-won't, Hawkins," said Harvey in a small voice.

Then suddenly all the stiffness that could possibly leave Hawkins' face left it. He smiled gently at

Harvey. "It isn't what you think, sir. You see, your kind mother and father, afraid that I might think the worst of you—which, of course, I could never do—confessed to me privately the reason for your wanting so desperately to keep the chickens at Moseley Mansion. And they explained the reason for the chicken march. It was all so I could have the eggs. Oh, sir!"

"Hawkins, I never wanted you to find out," blurted Harvey, "because of that gentleman's gentleman's pride stuff. You know!"

"I do indeed know, sir," said Hawkins, shaking his head ruefully. "Sometimes I confess that—er—gentleman's gentleman's pride stuff causes more difficulties than it does good, I'm afraid. But now with everything in readiness for the new owner, I believe the time has come for me to leave Moseley Mansion." Hawkins picked up the small black, leather suitcase sitting by the back door.

"Hawkins, I know you wouldn't let Mom and Dad drive you to the station, but couldn't I walk there with you?" Harvey pleaded.

"Thank you, sir, but I feel that a farewell at the station would be most difficult for us both. I would be most delighted, however, if you would accompany me to the gates of Moseley Mansion."

"I'd like that, Hawkins," said Harvey. "But, gee, do you have to leave so soon?"

Hawkins pulled a pocket watch from his jacket and consulted it. "It seems sir, that I do have some time left. How would you care to spend it?"

Harvey thought a moment. "Maybe we could go out together and visit the old place where our chickens used to be. I didn't want to see it alone, but I'd like to go with you, Hawkins."

"Oh sir, that—that would be simply splendid!"

XV

Going, Going, Gone!

Buzz! Buzz! Snap! Crackle! Buzz!

The sound exploded through the silence like firecrackers, all the way to where Harvey and Hawkins stood by the garages, gazing sadly at what was once the chicken yard and coop. Harvey started. "What was that, Hawkins?"

"If I am not mistaken, sir, it seems to be the sound of a loudspeaker system about to be put into use."

"Do you think the auction is starting?" asked Harvey.

"That is a distinct possibility, sir."

"Gee, if you don't have to leave right away, why don't we go over and watch. I'd like to find out who's going to buy Moseley Mansion. Boy oh boy, it better not be that Mr. Heister!"

"I'm afraid, sir, that my presence in full view of the audience would not be welcomed."

"Well, your presence doesn't have to be present in front of anything, Hawkins," said Harvey. "I mean, we can stand behind some of those big bushes, and nobody will see us. Anyway, even if you can't do anything about it, maybe you can still find out about that—uh—skulduggery stuff."

"I must admit, sir, that is a tempting idea. I might at least have the satisfaction of knowing my suspicions were not ill-founded."

"Boy, you sure would have that, Hawkins! So can we do it? Can we?" pleaded Harvey.

"Carry on, sir!" said Hawkins.

"Gee, Hawkins, look at all those people!" Harvey peered through the leaves of a dense, towering holly bush at the crowd gathered in front of Moseley Mansion. The chairs were all filled, and there were even people crowding around them, several rows deep.

"There does seem to be a large assemblage, sir," replied Hawkins. "Very surprising, indeed."

"Hey, look!" Harvey whispered excitedly. "There's Mr. Bunce from Bunce's Pet Store. And there's Charlie the barber—I mean, Sharles the hair stylist. And look over there. There's Uncle Doody and Aunt Bird, and even Uncle Doody's Cousin Theodore. Boy, I wonder what they're all doing here?"

"The news must somehow have circulated quickly, sir, and I would suspect they are here for the same reason as we are, to find out who the new owner of Moseley Mansion will be."

Buzz! Buzz! Snap! Crackle! Buzz!

The auctioneer tapped his microphone. "Testing! Testing!" Then he smiled a toothy smile at the audience collected before him, which included Mr. Heister and his friend in the front row. "My, we seem to have a surprisingly large crowd here today for the sale of this fine piece of property."

"I'll bet he *is* surprised, Hawkins!" Harvey whispered. "Hey, look, Mr. Bunce is raising his hand!"

"Sir," said the auctioneer, several more teeth appearing in his smile, "the auction hasn't started yet."

Mr. Bunce stood up. "Well, I just wanted to let you know a lot of us didn't come for the auction. We came to say good-bye to our good friend, Hawkins, who was unjustly ordered to leave this town. It looks like he's already left, so we thought we'd stick around to see what was going on."

Mr. Heister turned and threw Mr. Bunce the dirtiest look imaginable, but a lot of people in the crowd laughed and applauded. Harvey looked up at Hawkins and saw that his former gentleman's gentleman's face was working strangely, almost as if he were going to cry! Harvey looked away quickly.

"Harrumph! Harrumph!" The auctioneer cleared his throat noisily. "Before we proceed with the auction, I should like to say a few words about the Moseley Mansion estate. Ladies and gentleman, this big house you see behind me is—"

"Never mind all that nonsense!" Mr. Heister called out in an irritated voice. "Let's get on with the sale."

The auctioneer nervously displayed his teeth again in Mr. Heister's direction. "Harrumph! Harrumph! We will now proceed with the sale. The bid will start at one hundred thousand dollars. Who will make the first bid? One hundred thousand dollars, ladies and gentlemen."

Mr. Heister's friend raised his hand.

"The gentleman in the front row bids one hundred thousand dollars. Who will say one hundred twenty-five thousand? One hundred twenty-five thousand, anyone?"

One hundred thousand, as large a sum as that

was, was still far below what a house like Moseley Mansion with all its surrounding land should have sold for. But with Mr. Heister somehow arranging the sale to take place so suddenly, who was there prepared to buy except Mr. Heister's friend? Everyone looked at everyone else helplessly.

"If no one is prepared to bid higher for this magnificent property," said the auctioneer, "then it is going—going—go—"

A hand rose suddenly way at the back of the crowd, and a lady's voice rang out strong and clear, "I bid twenty-five cents!"

Mr. Heister's head whipped around furiously.

"I'm sorry, madam," said the auctioneer, "but this is a serious sale, not a joke."

"Well, I'm not joking. I bid twenty-five cents!" A tiny woman dressed in dark blue, and wearing a wide-brimmed hat with a veil drawn over her face, started marching up toward the front steps of Moseley Mansion. Behind her, huffing and puffing, trotted Mayor Paddle, his face pink with embarrassment. When the lady reached the auctioneer's podium, she whipped off her veil and turned to rivet Mr. Heister with a scorching stare.

A wave of whispers rolled over the audience. "Mrs. Moseley! Mrs. Moseley! Mrs. Moseley!"

"C-c-cousin Margaret!" stammered Mr. Heister, stumbling from his seat.

"Don't Cousin Margaret *me!*" snapped Mrs. Moseley. "Not after what *you've* done Percival Marmaduke Heister!"

Percival Marmaduke looked furtively over his shoulder, blanching at the sound of names he had clearly been trying to keep a dark secret.

"B-b-but you *are* my c-c-cousin, Cousin Margaret," he stammered.

"Second, three times removed, but not removed far enough in my opinion," retorted Mrs. Moseley. "I didn't like you when you were a little boy. I didn't like you when you were a bigger boy. And I don't like you very much now. You are *still* a weaselly brat, Percival Marmaduke!"

"B-b-but—"

"Never mind the buts," said Mrs. Moseley crisply. "I have just been having a long talk with my good friend Herbert Paddle, who admits to being very foolish in letting you take him over, especially when I convinced him that we liked him just the way he was." Scattered applause greeted this remark, and Mayor Paddle turned pinker than ever.

"Of course, I was foolish, too," continued Mrs. Moseley, "taking out a mortgage on Moseley Mansion until I could get my finances straightened out, and then allowing the money for that and the taxes to be sent to you, Percival. But how was I to guess that you would fail to make the payments so that Moseley Mansion would have to go on the block? I wouldn't have thought that even *you* could come up with such a wicked scheme!"

"I—I didn't do it so I could buy Moseley Mansion myself," whimpered Mr. Heister.

"No," agreed Mrs. Moseley grimly, "but you did it so Mr. Snipe could buy it and tear down this beautiful old house to put up rows and rows of—of *cracker boxes,* which he would have had the audacity to call homes. Yes, I've heard of you before, Mr. Snipe!" Mrs. Moseley pointed an accusing finger at the erstwhile buyer of Moseley Mansion, who quickly rose and slunk away.

"Fortunately," she said, "Mayor Paddle is also *President* Paddle of the Perpetual Paddle Savings and Loan Company, and we have just straightened the whole situation out. So this silly auction can come to an immediate stop!" Mrs. Moseley drew herself up to her full five feet and threw the auctioneer a fierce look.

"I—I thought it was for—for the good of the town," said Mr. Heister weakly.

"Not to mention a possible good to yourself, Percival Marmaduke," returned Mrs. Moseley. "Beautification and modernization, pfaw!"

"You aren't going to p-p-press charges, are you, Cousin Margaret?" asked Mr. Heister, now looking thoroughly frightened.

"Mayor Paddle, with my consent, is going to give you the benefit of the doubt, Percival Marmaduke, as we both think you may have been misled by Mr. Snipe. Mayor Paddle has agreed to let you stay on as his assistant, bearing in mind at all times that he is the one in charge of you, and not the other way around."

"Oh, thank you, Cousin Margaret," said Mr. Heister, almost in tears. "You know, I wouldn't have done any of this if I hadn't thought you wouldn't be—that is to say, you might never—"

"Might never return, is that it?" said Mrs. Moseley sharply. "You thought I was going to die, didn't you?"

"They—they *said* you were gravely ill," mumbled Mr. Heister, his face scarlet wih discomfort.

"And so I was!" said Mrs. Moseley. "I was fading away because I had lost my will to live—until I saw that article in the *Gazette* about the children's march and what was happening here in my absence. That snapped me back, I can tell you! Who knows what would have happened if I hadn't had that subscription to the *Gazette* sent to me by a kind and thoughtful person who could ill afford to send it, if what Mayor Paddle tells me is true about your misguided decision to cut off my butler's salary, Percival."

"I—I'm sorry, Cousin Margaret," stammered a

thoroughly beaten Mr. Heister. "I—I thought there wasn't enough money."

"Well, there was enough for *him,*" snapped Mrs. Moseley. "And, thank goodness, there is plenty now. I only hope I can find that good man and get him back here where he belongs. I assume he must have left, or he would be here now."

By this time, Harvey, still hiding behind the holly, was almost exploding out of his skin. Escaping Hawkins' restraining hand on his shoulder, he came bursting out of the holly bush. The package he was still carrying, to be presented to Hawkins at the gate, flew out from under his arm as he tripped on a root and went crashing to the ground yelling, "He's here, Mrs. Moseley! He's still here!"

Before an anxious Hawkins could even get to him to help him, Mrs. Moseley was hurrying up, with Mayor Paddle and Mr. Heister close behind.

As soon as she saw that Harvey had not been injured in his fall, Mrs. Moseley laughed out loud. "Well, this scene certainly does make me feel I am really home. Harvey Small tumbling out of the bushes, and Hawkins right behind to help him up. I should have guessed that you two would be together today."

"But we should not have been *here,* madam," said Hawkins. "This is most distressing indeed."

"It's my fault, Mrs. Moseley," Harvey blurted. "I

was the one who wanted to stick around and see who was going to buy Moseley Mansion. I talked Hawkins into it!"

"Yes, well, we all know how you can talk your former gentleman's gentleman into doing things, Harvey," said Mrs. Moseley, smiling. "Anyway, Hawkins, you had every right to be here. Your—er—banishment, as I understand it from Mayor Paddle, was not to begin until tonight. That, of course, as you probably gathered is no longer in effect, and you can stay right here, if you wish."

"Oh, madam!" said Hawkins.

"Wow!" said Harvey.

"By the way, young man," said Mrs. Moseley, addressing him. "I thoroughly enjoyed those pictures of you in 'Chuckle for the Day.' I believe they were what prompted Hawkins to send me the newspaper subscription."

"I am most terribly sorry, sir," said Hawkins. "I know how you felt about those pictures, but I suspected that they might give Mrs. Moseley a sorely needed—er—chuckle, so I took the liberty."

"That's okay, Hawkins," said Harvey. "Anyway, it was the newspaper that brought Mrs. Moseley back, and now I can give you this for a welcome-home present instead of a going-away present. It's worth being in 'Chuckle for the Day' for that!"

Harvey bent down to pick up the package he had dropped, and handed it to Hawkins.

"With all eyes on him, Hawkins carefully unwrapped the wrinkled paper from the long, flat package. Inside was the old *Rancho Hawkins* sign!

"Oh, *sir!*"

"I took it back out of my free-thing collection, Hawkins. We don't have our old chicken yard anymore, but I—I thought maybe you could hang it in your room."

"It would be an honor, sir."

"Well," said Mrs. Moseley, "Hawkins can hang it in the *new* chicken yard if he so chooses, Harvey."

"B-b-but, Cousin Margaret," interrupted Mr. Heister timidly, "chickens aren't allowed—"

"Oh, do be still, Percival! For your information, the ground we are now standing on used to be a farm, long before it ever became the Moseley Estate. One of the terms of the deed was that livestock *and* poultry could be raised here in perpetuity, which means *forever*. So much for your old chicken law, Percival Marmaduke!" Mrs. Moseley snapped her fingers under his nose. "And now I would like to adjourn to the house. Herbert, would you care to join us?"

"Thank you, Margaret, but—er—Percival Marmaduke and I," said Mayor Paddle with the greatest relish, "have a great many things to attend to at town hall. Come along, Percival! You have nothing else of importance to do here, I trust?"

"N-n-no, Your Honor."

"Then I want you to see at once about getting all those idiotic orange lampposts returned to their nice, original green."

"Y-y-yes, Your Honor."

"And I want you to get on the telephone and see about having those old windows at the school replaced.

"R-r-right away, Your Honor."

"And now about those new library books—"

"Well, so much for Percival Marmaduke Heister," said Mrs. Moseley. "And now, Hawkins, why don't you and Harvey take the car, go into town to Grandma Goody's Chocolate Shop, and load up with as much ice cream in assorted flavors and as many cookies as you can. I can see by all the smiles around here that you have a lot of friends who might like to help celebrate your return to Moseley Mansion."

"I would be delighted to do so, madam," replied Hawkins. "And if I might be allowed to say so at this time, it is—it is simply splendid to have you back again."

"Oh, pish tush, Hawkins," said Mrs. Moseley, looking pleased. "You can say anything you want to. Now, Harvey Small, why don't you push your eyeballs back in their sockets, close your jaw, and let us know what *you* think of all this."

"Oh—oh—oh!" gasped Harvey. *"Wow!"*

"If I might be allowed another comment, madam," said Hawkins, "I believe that that sums it up as well as anything could."

"It does indeed, Hawkins!" said Mrs. Moseley.